Carousel Worlds

Carousel Worlds

KIM DWYER

Copyright © 2021 by Kim Dwyer.

ISBN:	Softcover	978-1-6641-0598-0
	eBook	978-1-6641-0597-3

All rights reserved. No part of this book may be reproduced or transmitted in any form or by any means, electronic or mechanical, including photocopying, recording, or by any information storage and retrieval system, without permission in writing from the copyright owner.

This is a work of fiction. Names, characters, places and incidents either are the product of the author's imagination or are used fictitiously, and any resemblance to any actual persons, living or dead, events, or locales is entirely coincidental.

Any people depicted in stock imagery provided by Getty Images are models, and such images are being used for illustrative purposes only.
Certain stock imagery © Getty Images.

Print information available on the last page.

Rev. date: 05/27/2021

To order additional copies of this book, contact:
Xlibris
AU TFN: 1 800 844 927 (Toll Free inside Australia)
AU Local: 0283 108 187 (+61 2 8310 8187 from outside Australia)
www.Xlibris.com.au
Orders@Xlibris.com.au
826375

Dedicated to my loving mother Syb Jeffs

CONTENTS

Escape xi
Prologue 1

PART 1 CASSANDRA

Chapter 1   The Boy Next Door 7
Chapter 2   The First Shandy 14
Chapter 3   The Visit from Ray 17
Chapter 4   The Cousin 20
Chapter 5   Meeting the Parents 25
Chapter 6   Emotions 27
Chapter 7   A Pane of Glass 31
Chapter 8   Stranger 33
Chapter 9   The Baby Grand 34
Chapter 10 His Mother 37
Chapter 11 Cassandra 39
Chapter 12 Memories 42
Chapter 13 Ray 45
Chapter 14 School 46
Chapter 15 Shyness 49
Chapter 16 Cassandra's Choice 51
Chapter 17 Family Reunion 54
Chapter 18 New Love 58
Chapter 19 What to Wear! 61
Chapter 20 The Grunge Party 63
Chapter 21 The Outcome 66
Chapter 22 The Andersons 67
Chapter 23 Cassandra's Choice Accepted 70

PART 2 BRIDGET SKY ROSEWELL

Chapter 24 A Request 75
Chapter 25 Was That a *Unicorn?*...77
Chapter 26 Heaven 80
Chapter 27 "Why Us?"...82
Chapter 28 Goodbye..84
Chapter 29 To Sit and Talk..86
Chapter 30 The Replacement...88
Chapter 31 Learning and Communicating............................90
Chapter 32 Puzzle 92
Chapter 33 Less Time 93
Chapter 34 Friends, Fun, and Mandy....................................96
Chapter 35 Decision 99
Chapter 36 Daddy... 101
Chapter 37 The Angel... 104
Chapter 38 Mortal or God?.. 106
Chapter 39 Uncertain Future.. 107

PART 3 REALITY

Chapter 40 New South Wales 111
Chapter 41 Damen 114
Chapter 42 Time Flies... 115
Chapter 43 Angel... 117
Chapter 44 Angel's Way... 119
Chapter 45 Year 7 121
Chapter 46 Angel Chooses Earth (Well, *Robbie*) 123
Chapter 47 Martina 126
Chapter 48 Secrets 128
Chapter 49 Pressure 131
Chapter 50 Anger..133
Chapter 51 Her Middle Name 138
Chapter 52 Marie..142
Chapter 53 A New Best Friend..144

Chapter 54 Withdrawal 146
Chapter 55 Jake 148
Chapter 56 Martina's Note 150
Teenage Suicide 152
Chapter 57 Home Sweet Home 153

ESCAPE

In a safe and harmonious world
Lived Cassandra, a young girl.
Emotions reigned as events unfurled.

Cassandra met the fun-loving Bridget,
Who showed her other worlds existed.
To Heaven and Earth they visited.

A dark-haired girl was their mystery.
Her note wrote distressing history,
In the Blue Mountains west of Sydney.

PROLOGUE

In a safe and harmonious world
Lived James, an innocent young boy
He met beings from another world

"Cassie!" James aged four called out excitedly. His older sister came running out of the house to play. Their mother Valery walked out with cups of milk and home baked chocolate chip biscuits.

"When you two have finished chasing each other here's a morning snack for you," Valery laughed as her husband John joined in with the children running around playing Chasings.

A young dapple-grey horse named Desert Dancer looked over a nearby fence and whinnied. Valery patted him watching her happy family until John ran over and pulled her playfully into the game.

None of them suspected the dark days ahead.

A week later Cassandra and her mother walked outside their house carrying cups of water and watermelon cubes to have outside in the fresh air. John was working at the office.

"Jamie!" Valery called as she and Cassandra sat down at the outside dining table.

James didn't reply or show up.

"Maybe he's in the house, I'll go get him," Cassandra said before walking inside the house to look for him. She thought that maybe he wanted to play hide-and-seek. She couldn't find him.

An hour later Valery had called her husband home and was panicking because there was no sign of James.

******

James hid under his parents outside dining table waiting for his mother and sister to walk outside. He wanted to jump up and call out surprise to hear them laugh. As he sat still, he noticed a dark swirling image moving towards him making him think of a tornado he once saw in a book. Fascinated he felt spellbound, wondering how close it would come?

The darkness enveloped him, and he tried to cry out, but he couldn't find his voice. He passed out.

When James woke up, he was blind folded and strapped to a bed. A man's grating voice told him not to speak. James started crying in fear thinking the 'man' was more likely a monster. The man laughed a cruel laugh and told him he was in another world, but it wouldn't be for long. The man tried to explain to the four-year-old what was happening.

"Evil beings from another world were sick of your sister Cassandra's perfect, happy, harmoniously safe life." The man made a disgusting spitting sound. "They know that Cassandra is immortal and therefore protected. They know that the way to make Cassandra have some reality and pain would be to kidnap her beloved younger brother! You are mortal and vulnerable, unlike your sister."

James was scared because he didn't understand what was happening. He didn't know what words such as immortal or harmoniously meant. The man cast a spell to make the boy sleep.

When James woke up, he was in a nice, clean grey and white bedroom. He wasn't blind folded or strapped down. Beside the bed was a chest of drawers with a bottle of water and plate of hot stew for him. He grimaced but was so hungry he ate the terrible tasting stew. The room had an en suite with soap and a bath towel. A walk-in wardrobe had lots of clothing his size. Shelves were covered in many toys and books. He tried to open the door and window, but they were locked. He felt scared and alone but busied himself playing with toy cars on the floor.

Hours later he was so tired he went to bed and slept. The next day when he woke up, more of the terrible tasting stew was beside his bed but no drink. He ate all the stew wondering where his family were. For water he drank from the sink tap in the en suite. He coloured in, played with stuffed toy animals, and ran around the room holding a toy aeroplane above his head to make it 'fly' to pass the endless time alone.

This pattern kept repeating itself for days until two guys entered the room one evening when James was awake. They yelled at James because as soon as they opened the door he tried to run out. One of them held him and the other hit him in the stomach. James was left crying as the men left him alone with a small bowl of cereal and cup of milk. James started to leave bits of food under his bed, scared that the men would never come back again with enough food. He didn't know them, although one had called the other man Demon, which was likely a joke, but James didn't know for sure. He had heard the word demon once before in his young life and knew it was something to be terrified of.

As James grew older and taller, he started to think about ways of escaping. He thought the best way was to smash the window. He thought about using one of his heavy wooden drawers from his bedside chest. He knew that when the men visited him, they would then leave him alone for hours. He waited for the men to visit, yell at him for no reason and leave him, this time giving him raw carrots and out of date orange juice. Sighing he ate the carrots and flushed the juice down the toilet. Just then the toilet started to overflow! James thought to himself it would be hours before the mean men found out it was overflowing, until after the room was flooded and he was gone! Almost laughing for the first time in a long time, he smashed the window. Climbing out he cut his right arm on broken glass and ran up a long winding street bleeding. He was so weak after years of being inside without fresh air, sunshine or proper nutrition that he passed out on the street.

PART 1
CASSANDRA

CHAPTER 1

The Boy Next Door

A black beast squealed and struck a hoof against a stall door, impatiently waiting for his mistress to free him of otherwise comforting confines.

Cassandra walked down to the stables with confidence, smiling as she heard her horse call for her. Her long, straight hair was smooth and flowing over her shoulders. It was the beginning of school holidays, and she was reflecting on how fast the last school year had flown. Year 10 had been easy for the straight A student, and year 11 looked promising. She didn't make friends easily in school, as she was often gloomy and quiet, but her grades were excellent.

She lived in a luxurious, two-storey house with her parents, with a large, beautiful bedroom all to herself. This room had soft-pink walls and cream-coloured carpet plus a huge walk-in wardrobe. There was an en suite to her own black, marble bathroom and a very pretty, single pine bed with a patchwork quilt. Toy animals lined the bed: two teddy bears, a unicorn, a white seal pup, and a dolphin. Also in this bedroom were a desk, a computer, and a printer beside a pine bookcase filled with encyclopaedias, science fiction stories, and music books.

Her father was rich. Mr John Robert Condon was his name, and he was a tall, dark-haired, handsome lawyer. Her mother, Mrs Valery Jane Condon, was a successful author of science fiction books and worked part-time in a beauty salon. Neither had much time for their beautiful, fifteen-year-old daughter, but then Cassandra liked to be alone anyway.

The stables were a short walk from the back of the house. Upon reaching them, Cassandra stopped by the first stall to give her mother's horse, a true palomino mare named Golden Dream, a pat. In the next stall, her father's old, grey Andalusian gelding regarded her calmly. His name was Desert Dancer. He used to be dapple grey, but Des was turning white as he grew older.

In the third stall, Cassandra's Appaloosa gelding, Jet, scraped a hoof on the floor, reminding his mistress of his impatience. Cassandra leaned over his stall door and smiled at him, stroking his handsome face lovingly. He was black except for a blanket patch over his rump and a small, white star on his forehead. His coat was so shiny it appeared blue. Jet was now six years old; Cassandra had owned him since he was a yearling. They had a special bond.

Cassandra lifted down a bridle hanging outside Jet's stall. She opened the stall door, walked inside, and fitted the bridle on Jet, speaking softly the whole time. She then mounted his bare back and rode him out of the stables.

"Skywards, Jet!" she said.

Jet reared high on his hind legs. Cassandra knew he wanted to gallop freely, so she gave him his head. Her parents owned eight hundred acres of green, rolling hills at the foot of the magnificent Casyarna Mountains. Jet charged towards the mountains, his black mane flying as wildly as Cassandra's long, golden-brown hair.

After a while, Cassandra slowed Jet down and trotted him up and down hills, which was good exercise for the already muscular animal. A stream was nearby and became inviting on the hot summer day. Jet stepped into the swirling water while Cassandra patted his neck.

Jet's head shot up suddenly, ears swivelling in all directions.

"What's wrong, boy?" she asked. She then heard a noise behind her. She turned on Jet's back to see a young man watching her. He was holding the reins of a blue roan mare. Cassandra turned Jet around to face him.

"Hi," he said in a friendly voice.

"You're on private property," was the icy response he received.

"Your dad gave me permission, just to exercise my family's horses. My name is Ray. I moved in next door not long ago." Ray was relaxed and smiling easily with confidence.

Cassandra was looking at the blue roan Arabian mare. She was very pretty, with three white socks and a small star. The mare was in excellent condition.

Ray noticed Cassandra's interest in the mare but decided to comment on Jet instead. "That's a fine-looking horse you have there. Do you show him?"

"No."

Ray shifted uncomfortably. "What's your name?"

"Wouldn't you like to know?"

Ray sighed and tried to communicate with her again. "Well, there are more horses at home. Would you like me to show you?"

"I need to exercise my horse."

"You can ride with me—"

"No, my horse needs some work; your mare won't keep up!"

Ray looked puzzled for a moment. "You know, this blue roan can outrun a Thoroughbred! In fact—"

Cassandra urged Jet to walk out of the stream on to the grass, where he began to graze.

Ray was quiet for a moment, expecting the beautiful young girl before him to storm off any second. Then he thought he saw something in her eyes: *mischievousness*. He knew without a doubt that he was up for a challenge.

"OK," he said with a hint of a smile on his lips, "you're on for a race."

Cassandra looked off into the distance. "We will race from here to the bottom of the hill near the—"

"No, to the top of the hill and back," Ray interrupted, grinning now.

Cassandra wasn't used to people cutting her off in mid-sentence, but she let it pass without saying anything. She watched as Ray mounted the mare. Then the race began at a gallop.

They sped towards the hill that was near a large clump of rocks and bush. Cassandra didn't push Jet, and the mare didn't drop behind. As they raced back downhill, both horses picked up speed. On the stretch back to the stream, Cassandra noticed Ray was using spurs on the blue roan. The mare was sweating, and her nostrils were flaring. Frowning now, Cassandra urged Jet on. In a burst of speed, Jet reached the stream a few lengths ahead of the mare, sliding to a standstill.

Cassandra turned to face Ray. Jet was content. The mare was worked up and looked nervous.

Ray grinned at Cassandra half-heartedly. Before he could say anything, Cassandra asked in icy tones, "Why do you use spurs?"

Surprised, Ray replied, "Doesn't everyone?"

"Let me ride her," Cassandra stated, expecting to get her own way.

Ray felt a little indignant, never having met anyone like this before. He sighed. "You can ride her if you like, but first at least tell me your name!"

"Cassandra."

Ray felt attracted to this young beauty before him. She was an excellent rider—bossy, maybe, but that kept things interesting! He had enjoyed the mischievous look she had given him.

"You can ride Jet if you like. I don't know if he will let you, though. I'm the only one who has ever ridden him. What is this mare's name?"

"Lady Anna. You know, I think Jet will let me ride him. I've been riding since I was five!" Ray strode meaningfully over to Jet.

Cassandra shrugged. She started speaking softly to Lady Anna. She pulled the mare's saddle off and mounted bareback. Stroking the mare's neck, she sat still while watching Ray.

Ray spoke to Jet quietly. The Appaloosa had an alert look in his eye. As Ray tried to mount, Jet walked forward a few steps, not allowing Ray to get on. This was repeated a few times, and Cassandra tried not to grin. Finally, Ray found himself on the black back. Jet kicked up his heels and flattened his ears. Ray laughed. Jet pig-rooted again, higher than the first time. Then Ray used his spurs.

Jet snorted, dropped his head, and arched his back. He let go of some high bucks, but Ray stuck to him like glue. Cassandra could see what a good rider Ray was; perhaps Jet couldn't throw him after all. Then she saw Jet's eyes roll and nostrils flare. He rose up high and magnificent on his strong hind legs. As he came back down, he let loose with a mighty buck, twisting his body in mid-air and landing heavily on the ground with his legs braced.

This threw Ray off completely.

Ray landed on the ground in front of the blue roan's front hooves. The mare reared in fright and galloped for the hills with Cassandra lying low on her back. They sped only a short way before Cassandra managed to soothe her with a few words. Slowly and at ease, the mare cantered back to where Ray was sitting up, still in the same spot he had landed, apparently none the worse for wear. In fact, he was grinning.

"I can't believe what that black devil did! He's a one-girl horse!" Ray exclaimed.

Cassandra didn't reply. Her horse was fine and so was Ray, so she began to trot the mare in circles and figure eights. Lady Anna had lovely movement and a soft mouth.

After a while, Cassandra dismounted and said to Ray, "Please don't use spurs on her anymore; you don't need them." She mounted Jet.

Ray had a feeling she was about to leave and said, "Come over to my place. See our horses."

Even as he said this, Cassandra urged Jet to walk away.

Ray was left staring after her, not knowing what emotion gripped him in her wake. Quickly he saddled his horse, mounted, and caught up to Cassandra, who only glanced at him briefly.

"Can we ride together, Cassandra?" he asked tentatively. "I'd like to talk."

Cassandra was puzzled. Usually after spending this much time with her, other people didn't want to know her. She always preferred to be alone anyway, writing music in her room, reading books, or riding Jet. But this young man was good-looking and interested in her and seemed to love horses as much as she did! She was a fussy, rich, used-to-getting-her-own-way type of girl. But maybe she could give this guy a chance.

"Sure," she finally replied.

Ray was so surprised to hear her voice sounding friendly that he couldn't think of anything to say!

Cassandra stole another glance at him before relaxing on her horse's back.

Ray had short, dark-brown hair with a long fringe flopping over one eye. He was tall and lean with a light tan. He had a row of freckles across his face that made him look so—

Cassandra had to stop her thoughts and concentrate on talking to him! This was unusual for her!

"How long have you lived here?" Ray asked as the horses walked side by side.

"All my life," Cassandra answered. "I'll never leave either," she added firmly.

"It is beautiful up here. My family is from the flatlands. They worked so hard to be able to have the money to move here. I've just been accepted into the university down the road near the high school. I guess that's where you go to school?"

Their eyes met briefly. His were sky blue. Ray smiled warmly at her, which encouraged her to talk.

"Yes, I go to school there. I just finished year 10. What will you do in uni?"

"I will learn to be a vet. At first, I wanted to be a music teacher, but music is a hobby. What do you want to do when you leave school?"

Cassandra was quiet a moment, then she said, "A vet nurse."

Ray's face lit up, pleased they had things in common.

Cassandra had never seen someone's face light up so much over something small. She tried to suppress laughter, but it escaped! Furious with herself—she was normally well composed—she urged Jet into a canter towards Ray's place.

Ray was surprised. What was so funny? He cantered after her.

They reached the post and rail fence at the back of Ray's family property. Ray dismounted, opened a gate, and swept his arm in a gentlemanly gesture to allow Cassandra to ride through first. She slipped off Jet, walked through the gate, and allowed Jet to start grazing. The look on Ray's face was surprise yet again, but she simply said, "Jet won't go far. He comes when I whistle anyway."

Ray closed the gate and led the blue roan to a wash bay. They were quite some distance from the two-storey house that Cassandra had always admired. It was white with lots of roses growing all around. At the back was an in-ground swimming pool. There were honeysuckle and passionfruit growing close to the house.

Ray tried to make light conversation with Cassandra, but for some reason she had clammed up on him again. He lightly sprayed the mare with the hose. Cassandra stood nearby holding the tack.

"Here," he said, throwing her a bunch of keys. "There's the tack room over there, just put those—"

The keys came flying back at him! Cassandra put the tack down on the ground.

"What do you think this is, Ray? I'm not your slave."

Ray was stunned by the temper on this girl! He clenched his teeth.

Then suddenly Cassandra lunged forward and grabbed the hose! It slipped from his hands and she sprayed him in the face! He gasped and charged towards her. Cassandra dropped the hose in a sudden delightful panic and turned to flee.

Whump! She tripped and fell on the grass. Ray pounced and pinned her down. She couldn't move. He was laughing, but then he thought he saw fear in her eyes. Sometimes he forgot how strong he was!

Quickly he got up, also remembering he had only met this girl a short while ago. What was he doing? He stepped away from her feeling sheepish. "Sorry about that. I guess I lost my head. I—"

Then he saw it again! That mischievous look in her gorgeous eyes! What the! Why was he apologising? She started it! He was about to lose his temper, which was rare for him, when Cassandra picked up the tack and fallen keys. Casually she walked to the tack room while bestowing on Ray a dazzling "I'm innocent" smile.

All he could think of was how beautiful she was.

CHAPTER 2

The First Shandy

They stabled and fed Lady Anna then looked in the stalls at the other horses. There were five more. One Thoroughbred was a plain black gelding Ray's mother used for dressage. There were two black and white ponies with thick, shaggy manes. Cassandra thought they were adorable. They belonged to Ray's younger twin sisters. As both ponies vied for attention, Ray introduced them as Candy and Wanderer. There was also a long-legged, chestnut Arabian mare with a rather wild look about her. She showed the whites of her eyes and turned her tail end to them. Ray laughed.

"That's CC. She belongs to my brother Andrew. He's the only one who can get near her. He loves to ride her because she's so fast. He reckons he gets an adrenalin rush every time!"

Cassandra knew what that was like from riding Jet.

In the last stall was Ray's own horse, a buckskin with exceptionally large, dark-brown eyes. Ray cradled the horse's head in his arms and talked softly. The beautifully curved ears pricked forward to listen attentively. Cassandra took all this in, standing back slightly to give them space with a small, half smile playing on her lips. She waited patiently for Ray to remember she was there.

After a few minutes, he did. His face turned a light shade of red as he waited for Cassandra to say something smart, but she gave him a warm smile. He led the way out of the stables towards the house and offered her a drink.

Three dogs bounded up to them. Cassandra stopped to offer her hand to a brown and white boxer. The dog sniffed her hand and let her pat him. Then the other two dogs vied for her attention.

"The boxer is Petey," Ray said, "He was a stray that followed Andrew home. We put ads in the newspapers, but no one claimed him. The

Doberman is Reg. Big fella, isn't he? Great watchdog. The Labrador is Cinderella. My sisters named her after their favourite fairy tale."

They moved on towards the house, passed the fenced-off pool, and stepped onto the back veranda. Ray opened the back door and let Cassandra walk in before him. They entered a large sunroom filled with pot plants. There were a few chairs, a small tropical aquarium, and a yellow canary in a large wicker cage.

"Take a seat," Ray offered. "What will you like to drink?"

"Oh, just a—"

"Shandy? I'll be back in a minute."

Cassandra stared after him. Shandy? She was going to say an orange juice or water!

After a short while, Ray reappeared with two glasses. He handed one to her then sat in a chair opposite.

Cassandra took a tiny sip, then another. The liquid was nice and refreshing.

"What's in this?" she asked, embarrassed that she didn't already know.

Ray was surprised. "The shandy? You mean you don't know what's in a—?"

Cassandra's glare stopped him. He took a hasty swallow of his own drink. "It's just some light beer and lemonade. That's all. Not much beer. I hope you like it."

Cassandra loved it.

"It's not bad," she mentioned, trying to appear nonchalant.

A young boy sauntered into the sunroom. Cassandra thought she heard Ray mutter, "Oh no," into his glass.

"Hi there!" the boy said cheerfully as he plonked himself down in a chair beside Cassandra. "I'm Andrew. Who are you?"

Cassandra didn't answer. The boy was blond and looked no more than thirteen. She sipped her drink.

Andrew looked across at Ray.

"Got ya self another babe. Hey mate, but what happened with your other chick? The redhead? She was hot! Why—"

Andrew said a few swear words Cassandra had never even heard before.

Ray calmly leaned down to put his drink safely on the floor. He then lunged forward and grabbed Andrew's arm, *hard*.

Andrew whimpered. "Let go, Ray! I didn't do nothing wrong! I won't swear again. I promise!"

Ray led the boy to another part of the house. Cassandra could hear Ray having firm words with the boy.

She finished her drink and was planning to leave when two girls skipped into the room. They stared at her in surprise.

Cassandra couldn't tell them apart. They were identical twins. Both had long, dark-brown hair to their waists and freckles on their faces. Even their clothes were the same; Cassandra wasn't keen on that idea when it came to twins.

"Hi," said one of them. "I'm Jessica, and this is Alex. Who are you?"

"Cassandra," she replied politely, putting down her empty glass.

"How did you get here?" Jessica asked.

"By Jet, and now I'm leaving."

Fed up with waiting for Ray, Cassandra walked out the back door, then ran across the property to the fence where Jet was waiting. She flung her arms around his neck, and it felt good to hug her beloved horse. Again, she just wanted to be alone. Ray had stirred all kinds of feelings within she had never felt before. She mounted Jet and rode off into the hills.

CHAPTER 3

The Visit from Ray

Over the next couple of days, Cassandra spent time playing music or lunging Jet in a round yard near the stables. Until early one morning her mother Valery shook Cassandra awake, saying, "Hurry. Downstairs there's someone here to see you!"

Cassandra groaned; she had been hoping to sleep in for once. She looked up to see her mother's smiling face.

"It's that nice boy from next door. How about getting out of bed, perhaps with a smile for today?"

Cassandra responded by pulling a face. "Tell him to—"

"Cassandra! Get up and come downstairs." Valery walked to the bedroom door, stopped, and said, "Put on something nice for a change, perhaps different to a T-shirt," then left.

Cassandra got out of bed and took a quick shower. She felt sheepish for running out on Ray the other day and wasn't so sure she wanted to see him again so soon.

She put on a clean new pair of black jodhpurs and a light, pretty blouse that had a flowery pattern (to please her mother). As she pulled on her riding boots, she thought this might give Ray the hint she wanted to go horse riding rather than hang out with him and her parents all day. As she walked down the stairs, she expected to see Ray and her mother standing near the front door. Instead, she heard them laughing and talking with her father in the dining room. She made her way there.

Her parents were seated at the dining table with Ray, having cinnamon toast and sipping hot tea. Usually breakfast was a quiet, solemn affair in their household. She stood watching jealously as Ray had a joyous time talking with her parents.

After a while, her father noticed her.

"Here's my dear daughter now," he said grandly, causing Cassandra to give him an odd look. Her father would normally never sound grand! "Come sit with us."

Cassandra sat at the table averting her eyes and not seeing Ray's light up at the sight of her. She poured herself some tea and started to nibble on a piece of toast.

Valery said, "Good morning, Cassandra. Have you forgotten your manners?"

Cassandra thought she would die of embarrassment. "Good morning," she said quickly.

Ray cleared his throat nervously. "Good morning, Cassandra. I was wondering if you would like to accompany me to, uh. Well, there's going to be an arts and crafts festival in town today. Would you be interested in joining me?"

Cassandra nearly spilled her tea. *He was asking her on a date?* After she ran out on him? What was with this guy? "I wanted to go horse riding today," she said shyly.

Her mother looked disappointed but didn't say anything.

Ray got to his feet. "Well, OK. I wasn't sure if you'd be interested anyway. If you have other plans—" His voice trailed off.

"Just go," her mother said quietly. Her daughter was alone so much, and Ray was so nice. It would be good for Cassandra to have a friend for a change!

Cassandra glared fiercely in embarrassment at her mother then got up from the table, excused herself (borne from long practice), and fled out of the house. She went straight to the horses' feed shed to sit on a bale of hay to brood just like when she was small.

After a few minutes, Ray appeared. He leaned in the frame of the open doorway. "Hi," he said.

She gave him a small, funny smile.

"What was that all about?" he asked.

Shrugging, she apologised. "I'm sorry, Ray. My parents seem to think they can push me around, and I really did plan on going horse riding today."

"Well, so did I. I'm not interested in the festival really. I just thought you might be and would like to go, but hey, how about riding into the hills together?"

Cassandra was surprised. This guy really seemed to like her! She looked up at him. He was smiling at her with confidence, and he looked so good. He smoothed his fringe off his forehead with his fingers, and as it flopped back down again, he walked over and helped her up.

Together they rode into the hills in the morning sunlight, not knowing that Valery stood watching from the back door of the house, a pleased smile on her face.

Chapter 4

The Cousin

Cassandra and Ray were comfortable in each other's company that day riding together. Cassandra rode Jet, and Ray rode his buckskin, Sun Seeker.

At first Cassandra didn't talk much. Ray was open natured and loved to talk. It seemed to him Cassandra didn't enjoy people getting to know her, almost as if she had built a wall around her heart no one could get past. But as the sun climbed the sky, she started to relax and talk more.

Later that morning, they dismounted to let their horses pick at the grass and take a break. Ray stretched out on his side, and Cassandra sat near him cross-legged.

After a moment of silence, she asked, "Ray, was what Andrew, that blond boy at your place the other day, said true? About the other girl?"

Ray sat upright. "No!" he said angrily. "He just likes to tell lies to torment me. I'm sorry you met him the other day."

"Is he always so loud and obnoxious?"

Ray sighed. "Yes."

"Then why does the chestnut mare let him near her? She looked intelligent but rather bad-tempered as though she needs someone quiet and gentle to tame her. How can she let that boy near her?"

Ray looked at the girl before him in puzzlement then started laughing. Cassandra stared at him.

"No, that wasn't my brother. That was my cousin Andy you met. He just has the same name as my brother. They are opposite. My cousin is a spoiled brat, staying with us for the holidays. CC won't go near him. Believe me. Come to think of it, Andy won't go near our horses since Jess's pony bit him."

"Where was your brother?"

"He was out shopping with my father. His sixteenth birthday is coming up and he wants a computer. He's always using Dad's, sometimes for hours. He wants to be a computer programmer someday."

"And your sisters?"

"Jess and Alex? What about them?"

"What do they like?"

"Horses and Barbie dolls."

Ray lay back down.

Cassandra watched the horses. Jet shook his black mane, lifted his head, and looked back at her. He walked over to where she was sitting to place his soft muzzle on her shoulder. Forgetting Ray, Cassandra spoke soft words to her horse.

A few moments later, it was her turn to go red when she noticed Ray watching her. She stood up hastily to mount her horse, but Ray said, "Oh no, you don't," and pulled her gently down on the grass.

"You can't keep running away, Cassandra. I want to spend the whole day with you!"

Slowly the uncomfortable feeling left Cassandra. The rest of the morning passed pleasantly. Not long after midday, they headed back to Ray's house for lunch.

Cassandra sat at the dining table watching Ray in the kitchen opposite.

"I can make the best hamburgers this side of the Casyarna Mountains!" Ray announced. "Would you like a drink while you wait?"

Cassandra smiled. "A shandy would be nice."

Ray gave her a glass then started making lunch. It was quiet for a while then Ray's cousin Andy walked in. He stared at Cassandra. She stared back.

"What? You back again? How can you stand this loser?" Andy asked, gesturing with his thumb over his shoulder at Ray.

Cassandra saw Ray turn a light shade of red. She glared at the boy. "What's your problem, you self-centred little brat? Jealous?"

Both Andy and Ray were shocked.

"What did you call me? You cow! Why—"

Ray grabbed the back of Andy's shirt collar, dragged him out of the dining area, and put him out the back door. Cassandra had a clear view of the door and saw Andy press his open mouth up against the glass door, stick both his fingers up, and roll his eyes. Ray left him there and went back into the kitchen.

"He acts like such a brat sometimes. He's so spoiled his own parents can't handle him. After these holidays, they want to send him to a boarding school. I wonder if they will. I mean they meant it as a joke, but still!"

"Why is he staying here?"

"His father is abroad on business, and his mother is looking after a sick relative. They asked my parents if it was OK for him to stay here. They said yes, and so now we all have to suffer."

Suddenly they heard a scream from the backyard. Ray rushed outside, Cassandra right behind him. She stood on the back veranda to see what was happening, sipping a shandy.

Ray's twin sisters had brought some teddy bears and Barbie dolls outside to play with, and Andy had decided to join them. He had thrown a white bear on the roof of the house. Western Barbie and Beach Barbie were floating in the pool. Alex was screaming because Andy was trying to take a chocolate-brown coloured bear from her hands, but she had a very firm grip. Jess was watching tearfully.

Ray ran at Andy and in a flying tackle pinned the boy down.

"Get off me!" Andy yelled.

"I want you to apologise to my sisters, then you stay away from them!"

Andy turned his head to look at the twins. "Sorry, gals," he said sarcastically.

"Say it like you mean it!" Ray said angrily, shaking him roughly.

"Ow! Stop it! I'm sorry!" the boy cried.

"OK," said Ray, letting Andy up. "Now I want you to go and think about growing up for a change."

Andy took two steps away, poked his tongue out at Ray, and ran off towards the stables.

"Come back here!" Ray yelled as he took off after him.

Andy ran in a half circle and started heading for the house. The dogs, Reg, Petey, and Cinderella, appeared from nowhere and raced towards him. Andy swiftly changed direction to avoid the dogs and ran past the twins.

He grabbed the forbidden teddy bear as he swept by and had the dogs, Ray, and the twins after him. *He's a fast kid. That's for sure,* Cassandra thought as she watched in amusement.

Not far from the pool fence, Andy slipped and fell. Reg jumped on him gleefully, and Petey began barking.

Ray stood back and watched with his sisters. Cassandra couldn't help laughing.

Finally, Ray called off the dogs. Andy looked tired, his hair and clothes a mess. Ray helped him up and walked him back to the house. As they went inside, Cassandra saw a teenage boy walk out of the stables. The sound of a neighing horse and something being knocked over made him run back inside.

Curious, Cassandra went to investigate.

She found him in CC's stall with one arm around the horse's neck, stroking the mare's lovely face.

He heard Cassandra as she walked over to the stall and looked up. He was a younger version of Ray with glasses. He was just about to say something when Ray appeared beside her.

"There you are," Ray said to Cassandra cheerfully. "I finally put that cousin in his place. Hi, Andrew. Have you met Cassandra?"

Andrew shook his head and smiled shyly.

"How did CC go today?" Ray asked.

"Faster than Lightning! She outran my friend Steve's horse, the ex-racehorse! She left him for dust."

Ray laughed. "Well, I guess Steve can't brag about his horse anymore."

"She sure showed them."

"What was that sound before when you walked out of here?" Cassandra asked.

Andrew didn't answer. Ray ginned.

"CC never wants Andrew to leave her," Ray explained. "Starts a fuss every time he walks away. I don't know what she sees in you, Andrew," he teased.

Andrew grinned at his older brother. "It's just my good looks, charm, and personality, Ray!"

Ray laughed. "Modesty too! Come on and have lunch with us."

They went back to the house and Ray poured Cassandra another shandy. The twins came in, grabbed some sandwiches that Ray gave them, and then disappeared into the lounge room to watch TV. Cassandra couldn't tell which twin was Jess and asked Ray.

"The one on the left was Jess," he said, as if that had been obvious.

They sat down to a nice lunch.

CHAPTER 5

Meeting the Parents

The hamburgers were delicious as promised. Cassandra thought Andrew was sweet and had a great sense of humour. After lunch he went to use his dad's computer.

Cassandra felt like another drink.

Ray grinned at her. "Sure, I'll get you another shandy."

They sat at the table for another hour talking about animals and veterinary procedures that they were both so interested in. Ray noticed that Cassandra was completely relaxed and rather talkative. He realised how much she had had to drink, and it wasn't light beer this time. He waited for her to empty her glass then suggested a walk in the fresh air.

Cassandra stood up and fell right back into her chair, laughing. He stood to help her stand up, his arm around her small waist, and then his mother walked in with an armful of shopping.

"Hello, dear. Could you help me with this?" she asked.

Ray faltered. "Uh, sure, Mum."

Cassandra sat down again. She felt funny but happy. She looked up at Ray's mother. She was a tall woman with a short, stylish haircut that suited her pretty face. A certain warmth and confidence radiated from her. She smiled warmly at Cassandra.

"Hello. You must be the girl from next door. I've met your parents. Cassandra, isn't it?"

Cassandra only smiled, not trusting her voice to speak.

Ray was nervous. He liked Cassandra a lot and wanted his parents to like her as well. He knew Cassandra was tipsy and feeling uncomfortable about it.

Ray's father walked in and gave his wife a kiss on the cheek. He began to help put away groceries then noticed Cassandra sitting quietly at the table. He gave her a wide, cheerful smile.

"Hi there! Ray, aren't you going to introduce us?"

"Dad, this is Cassandra from next door. Cassandra, my dad."

"Just call me Bryan. My lovely wife here is Gabrielle. Welcome to our humble home!"

Ray groaned as he put groceries away. He stopped to turn and look at Cassandra. She was just sitting there.

Cassandra felt tired. When it suddenly went quiet, she looked up nervously. Ray and his parents were waiting for her to say something. She smiled weakly.

"Hiiiii," she drawled, and then she blushed.

Bryan and Gabrielle glanced at each other.

"She's shy," Ray defended Cassandra before walking back to the table to sit beside her.

"Well, looks like the two lovebirds want to be alone," Bryan said with a grin so much like Ray's. Ray groaned again.

Gabrielle finished putting the groceries away. "Well, it's nice to meet you, Cassandra. Hope you come over here again soon. You're always welcome. Come on, dear." Gabrielle took her husband's arm. "Let's leave them alone."

They walked away into the lounge room.

Ray and Cassandra sat very still for a minute then went out of the house into the backyard, laughing until their sides hurt.

"I don't think I made a good first impression!" Cassandra laughed.

They sat together under the shade of a huge tree, talking about horses. Cinderella joined them. They lazed away the afternoon simply talking about horses.

Ray tried to get Cassandra to open up about her home life for he had seen the tension between Cassandra and her parents, and he was curious about it. However, she swiftly changed the subject back to horses.

CHAPTER 6

Emotions

When Cassandra arrived home that night, her parents were waiting at the dinner table for her. Usually dinner was a little later in the evening, but there were her parents already at the table, which was set with cutlery and crockery already. That was usually Cassandra's chore.

Cassandra sat down quickly, half expecting dinner to be a quiet, solemn affair the same as on other nights, but her parents wanted to talk.

Valery cleared her throat. "Did you have a nice day, Cassandra?" she asked.

"Yes," Cassandra replied, looking down at the pink salmon and steamed vegetables smothered in white sauce on the expensive, gold-rimmed, white plate. Salmon was her favourite dish, a rare delicacy this side of the Casyarna Mountains. She wondered what the occasion was.

"You know, Cassandra, we never get to talk much," her father said, "and your mother and I have been thinking about how fast you are growing up. The fact you have spent time with Raymond means a lot to us. You always wanted to be alone, never bringing friends home from school. It's not right."

Valery placed her hand over her daughter's hand. "We both love you so much," she said gently.

Cassandra saw the truth in her mother's eyes.

"I know we don't say that often. I know we don't show you affection often."

"But you turn away from us," her father continued. "You started to shut people out a long time ago. Ever since—" His voice trailed off.

Valery took a deep breath.

"Honey, you know you mean the world to both your father and me. We need to tell you something that we think you may have forgotten or that might stir up memories you have hidden deep. You have a brother one year younger than you. His name is James, and you used to adore each other. When you were three, you would do anything to make him smile. You—"

"He had a nice smile," Cassandra suddenly whispered, staring down at her plate.

"Yes," her mother said softly, "you used to smile back then yourself. When you started having piano lessons at the age of five, James would sit and clap for you. In his eyes, you made no mistakes. He used to look up to you. But then—" Valery's eyes welled up in tears.

"He died," Cassandra said flatly, her face a mask.

"No," her father said after a shocked silence. "He didn't die as we believed."

Cassandra's head shot up, her eyes piercing her father's. "What do you mean? You told me he died! You sent me to Grandmother's for a week, and she told me the same thing! He had an illness, and now he's dead!"

Valery lowered her head, letting tears fall freely.

John went red before speaking. "After what happened to James, you withdrew into yourself and started to change. You used to be happy and affectionate, until James was taken. He's not dead, Cassandra. He was kidnapped when he was only four, and we haven't spoken to or seen him since. While you were at your Grandmother's house, we were a mess. We had the police search for him—to no avail. There wasn't anything anyone could do! To this day, we still think of our son and miss him. We received a note in the mail saying he was dead, and we believed it. Investigations and searches lasted for months and months, but no one could find him. We had to get on with our lives, return to work, and continue raising you. You had withdrawn so completely! You never did cry but hid your emotions behind a calm mask forever on your face. It's not healthy to hide emotions all bottled up within."

After a short silence, dinner untouched, Cassandra asked calmly, "Is he still alive?"

Her father handed Cassandra an envelope. Her hands starting to shake she took out a letter. Questioningly, she looked up at her father.

He nodded his head. "It's from James."

"He sent photos as well." Her mother handed Cassandra the photos.

The first photo showed a lean, teenage boy standing outside an enormous brick building blocking out the sky with many barred windows. He was standing on concrete. It wasn't a close up, and Cassandra couldn't make out his facial expression.

Another photo showed him sitting on a neatly made bed, both his feet on the floor. He was leaning forward and looking directly at the camera with dark eyes. His gaze was unsettling.

Cassandra put this photo down and looked at the last one.

This showed a close up of his face. He had the same angular good looks as their father with the same dark eyes and hair. He was not smiling, his face was calm, yet there seemed something odd about the photo Cassandra couldn't put a name to. She knew James would only be fourteen, but this photo seemed to make him older. Shakily she put the photo down and unfolded the letter.

> Cassandra,
>
> I don't know if you remember me. I am your brother James. I was taken from our parents' house when I was four years old by complete strangers. I don't know if you've been told otherwise.
>
> I live at an orphanage several miles from where you live. When I was kidnapped, it was by two people who abused me. I ran away from them when I was ten. All I wanted was to find my family again.
>
> I met up with an old man who took pity on me because I was sick and uneducated. I wanted to live with him, but he brought me to this orphanage. I have since found out he has passed away.
>
> At this orphanage, I have learned to read and write and began a search for my family. The people working here helped me.
>
> I remember a big house, you playing a piano, and a grey horse in a stable.

I was wondering if you would like to see me again. I would like to hear from you. Below is the address of the orphanage. Please write soon.

Your brother,
James

Cassandra's heart was beating fast and loud. She didn't realise she was holding her breath until she had to let it out. Slowly she put the letter down and looked up at her parents' worried, almost fearful eyes. She knew they were hurting badly just like she was. She tried to imagine what it would be like to be a parent and have a beloved son kidnapped. Suddenly tears sprang to her eyes. The emotionless mask slipped from her face and she shook as her tears flowed.

CHAPTER 7

A Pane of Glass

A week later, Cassandra's father turned his favourite car, a green Jaguar, into Oak Lane, hands shaking slightly. His wife was pale under her freshly applied makeup, and his daughter sat tensely in the back seat. The car cruised serenely and rolled to a stop outside an enormous building with barred windows. Slowly they got out of the car to walk across a lush green lawn, barely noticing the beautiful fish pond and fountain in the centre.

On the entrance door to the building, in white lettering, were the words "East Casyarna City Orphanage," and in small print underneath was "Founded by Ms Goldwell."

The reception area was pleasant and rather dull. The receptionist was a plump, older-looking woman who smiled at them dutifully as they approached her desk. John asked about seeing his son James. The woman walked out from behind the desk and led them through a side door back outside.

The building itself was shaped like a horseshoe around a court with beautiful gardens. It was on a large property that had an agricultural plot and an oval for playing sports.

Cassandra took all this in quickly. She was feeling sick from nerves and excitement that had been building up all week, a solitary week. She stepped after her parents as the receptionist led the way round the side of the semicircular building and in through a sliding door. They walked up two flights of stairs and stopped outside a wooden door with the number 28 painted on it in white. The receptionist knocked twice.

A red-haired teenage boy opened the door and stuck his head out with a wide grin showing off even white teeth.

"Hi, Ms Carter," he said to the receptionist. "Looking for James?"

Ms Carter opened the door wider, and they all walked into the room. James was sitting on his bed, same as in the photo he had sent to them. Slowly his eyes met with Cassandra's. Cassandra's eyes dropped to the floor almost immediately. James's perceptive gaze saw straight through her, and she trembled. She had been expecting a little brother, not this stranger who seemed to see straight through her.

He seemed to read her on the spot, but how could he? He seemed so much older than her, but he was younger.

She felt like a pane of glass.

CHAPTER 8

Stranger

On the way back home, Cassandra sat nervously in the front seat of the Jaguar while her mother sat with James in the back, clasping his hand.

James was quiet yet polite to his mother, who rattled on incessantly of how happy she was to have him with them again. He felt so nervous. Cassandra had given him an odd reaction upon meeting, and she wouldn't meet his eyes! His mother's nervous talk was unsettling. He felt he didn't know these people, yet they were his family.

Valery. His mother was nervous but looked like the type of person to normally be confident and in control. She held his hand as if afraid to let go.

John. His father had been straightforward with James and shaken his hand. James had liked that. It had been a shock at first to see how much they look alike.

Cassandra. His sister. So beautiful yet untouchable. One look at her and he knew she wasn't comfortable around people. He had felt her trying to withdraw from him at the orphanage, and a few expressions had crossed her face. Expectancy, fear, realisation. Expecting what? Fear? He would never harm her!

Had she suddenly realised, just like himself, that they were complete strangers these days? He had agreed to live with *complete strangers?*

CHAPTER 9

The Baby Grand

As the Jaguar headed towards the house along a shaded, tree-lined drive, James looked out at the size of his new home. *Huge.* A house that was two storeys high with rolling green hills for miles around. A golden horse turned out to graze in a paddock shook her creamy mane and turned her head to placidly watch the family arrive home. Butterflies flapped brightly coloured wings in the mid-morning sun, paying no heed to two small kittens frolicking nearby. Myriad flowers grew in a large, circular section cut out of the middle of a paved area in front of the house and triple garage. John smoothly parked his prized Jag.

James only had one bag. He carried it up the front steps to the house with Valery clinging to his arm. John opened the door then said, "Valery, why don't you and Cassie go inside and prepare morning tea? We'll be there in a minute."

Valery was reluctant to let go of her son's arm, so Cassandra pulled her inside. They disappeared in the direction of the kitchen.

John looked at James and smiled. "James, I know this won't be easy."

Father and son regarded each other calmly. "You can call me John if you find that easier."

James shifted from one foot to the other. He turned his eyes to the kittens, tumbling in their play in the flowers. As one batted soft paws at the other, James looked back at his father, who he had been longing to have in his life for the past ten years.

"I would like to call you Father," he said hesitantly, "if that's OK."

John was surprised but happy to hear this. He placed a comforting hand on his son's shoulder.

"That would be fine. Remember we've all missed you. We are here for you, and we're all glad you've come back home, *son.*"

James nodded. They walked in through the front door to the entrance room. James nearly dropped his bag in shock. This place was massive! He had forgotten so much about the first four years of his life here!

Beautiful, polished, wood floors, oriental rugs, brilliant paintings of landscapes, and horses—were his parents loaded with money *or what?*

John casually took off his coat, hung it in a small closet near the door, and turned to see James's surprised, white face staring at a painting of a splendid dapple-grey horse.

"This way to the kitchen, James," he said cheerfully as he led the way.

James tore his eyes away from the paintings and slowly started to follow John.

John had stopped and was standing beside—

"Cassandra's piano!" James exclaimed as his face lit up. This he remembered. The curves of the baby grand piano, three gold foot pedals shining softly, and ebony and white keys just waiting to be played.

James sat on the black leather piano stool. Gently he laid a hand on the keys, pleasant memories flooding him. Cassandra's music lessons.

John walked into the kitchen and embraced his wife.

Cassandra had just switched the kettle on to boil and was reaching for the biscuit jar when her father said, "I think James would like to see you, Cassandra. He's at the piano."

Cassandra's hand stilled and she turned to see her father's happy smile. She walked out of the kitchen to join James, her hands clasped together nervously.

"Would you like me to play?" she asked.

"Please," he said simply, standing up.

Cassandra sat down and easily ran her fingers up and down in a crescendo of scales all neatly timed. She then started to play a piece of music she had written herself, a classical piece in the key of F major. James was caught up in the music and wishing he could play piano too.

Cassandra relaxed into her desire of playing music. She played many different songs before realising she was starving, and that James probably was too. She finished the song she was playing.

James clapped for her. She knew it was because he was remembering back to when they were children and he used to clap for her when she practised.

"That was great!" James said. "I wish I could play."

Cassandra dropped her eyes shyly. "I can teach you."

"I'd like that."

They walked back into the kitchen together.

CHAPTER 10

His Mother

John held Valery close and they swayed gently back and forth in the kitchen while listening to their talented daughter playing piano. Valery calmed down within her husband's arms. She smiled warmly, feeling their happiness at their son's return.

By the time the two teenagers had entered the kitchen, their parents were chatting and dishing up thick beef soup, white bread rolls, and herb vegetable dishes. Cassandra set the table and prepared hot tea.

James couldn't remember eating so well. The rolls were delicious, especially when dipped in the soup. He ate quickly and finished eating first. Valery served him seconds without any hesitation, and James accepted.

After lunch, Valery asked James to go upstairs with her. They walked through the spacious lounge room towards the stairs. James took in the fireplace, large windows, lace curtains, and comfortable-looking lounge chairs.

There were framed family photos hanging on the wall leading up the staircase. One was of his parents on their wedding day. Valery wore an elegant, flowing, white dress with tiny pearls dripping delicately around its hem. John, ever practical, wore a black suit. He was gazing lovingly into his bride's eyes.

Other photos showed either him or Cassandra or both. He saw how Cassandra's eyes were happy in her childhood photos and solemn in her teenage photos.

They reached the top of stairs and Valery led him to his old bedroom. They sat on the bed side by side. There was a chest of drawers, a large wardrobe, and windows looking out over the property. The ceiling and carpet were white. The walls were rich blue, matching the colour of the bed quilt.

"We've missed you so much and never stopped thinking about you," Valery began. "The most painful experience of my life was losing you. I'm so glad you're home, and I'm going to try to have a normal mother-son relationship. But I need to know how you feel."

James replied, "I am glad to be home, but I don't know how to feel right now. I have missed you so much it hurts—" His voice trailed off.

Valery could see the pain his eyes. "Of course, you need time to get used to things. Just remember I'm here for you. We all are."

She hugged him close, and James tensed at first, not used to sudden affection. Then he returned the hug, knowing and loving Valery as his mother.

CHAPTER 11

Cassandra

A day later, Valery and James again sat in James's bedroom together. The sun streamed in to shine on a large, wooden toy chest near the window. James had a lot of memories wrapped up in that chest he had yet to explore, but for now, his full attention was on his mother. She said, "We all searched for you, James. The police searched for months. Then we received a message you were dead, but there was no trace to lead us to the kidnappers. Your sister loved you so much we didn't know how to tell her that you may have been murdered. We told her you died because of an illness." Valery took a deep breath, tears brimming. "We lied to protect her. We always wanted her safe. After losing you, we couldn't bear to lose another. She has been spoiled, indulged, and sheltered. She became terribly withdrawn when you went missing."

James moved closer to his mother to take her hand. "Nothing is your fault," he stated clearly, with direct eye contact. "You've raised her as best a mother can. Anyone can see the intelligence in Cassandra, and she's fine."

He paused.

"Hearing Cassandra play the piano brought back memories of how close we were. She is going to teach me to play. She is talented."

At that, Valery looked surprised.

"What?" James asked.

"Cassandra is normally a loner! I'm so glad she is going to spend time with you."

They sat together a long time getting to know each other again before Valery left to give James some time to himself.

James walked over to the window and looked out over the green land, the mountains in the distance, and the blue sky that stretched forever. All this beautiful space for him to enjoy! His mind was a whirl of emotion as his thoughts ran wild with all that was happening in his life.

"James?" a soft tentative voice caused him to turn from the window.

Cassandra stood in his bedroom doorway, her stomach full of butterflies.

James looked at her steadily, seeing her nervousness.

"Come in," he invited.

Cassandra stepped inside. She wasn't sure why she had come to James; something had drawn her to him.

She could remember how close they were, how she hadn't liked being an only child. She wanted to be close to her brother again, but being near James now was so different. He wasn't an adoring little brother anymore. Sure he was younger, but he seemed *older*. She thought about how she had helped their mother look after him when they were little, so she could play "mother."

Now James was ten years older. He had survived without family for ten years! As if he would need her now!

James stared as his sister, without a word, turned, and fled. He stood still in surprise for a moment. What was she running from? Then he raced out after her, down the stairs and out the back door to the stables where he heard her crying. He slowed to a walk. He found her hugging a black horse around the neck.

Jet turned his ears towards him.

James stood uncomfortably. He ran a hand through his short, cropped, black curls. He didn't know what to do or say. After a moment, he stepped forward and stroked Jet's handsome face.

Slowly Cassandra calmed down.

"I'm sorry," she whispered.

"Don't be," James replied.

Cassandra told James that she didn't know how to act or feel around him. She felt childish and stupid telling him but was glad to get it off her chest.

James replied, "I just want your friendship, Cassandra, someone to talk to. Just be yourself and don't change for me. We need to get to know each other again."

Cassandra smiled.

"How about a piano lesson?" he added.

Cassandra smiled in surprise. He did need her after all!

CHAPTER 12

Memories

The next fortnight passed pleasantly. Cassandra started giving James piano lessons and found he picked up on the lessons quickly. John was busy with work, and Valery was busy writing science fiction stories. Her books were well known, and some were bestsellers.

No one asked James about his past. No one commented on the scar running down his right arm or the fact he often stored or hid food under his bed. Sometimes James would go for long walks for hours at a time to be alone. His family gave him his space, and this he appreciated.

One sunny day, he was out walking along the fence line of his parents' property when he saw a boy about his sister's age riding a bony horse. James leaned up against the fence to watch.

The boy leaned low on the horse's back as they galloped by, mane and tail streaming. The boy turned the horse, slowed, and cantered in circles. After slowing to a walk, he noticed the dark-haired stranger. He urged his horse towards him.

James stared at the long-legged chestnut approaching him. He wasn't familiar with horses, but he could see the wild look in her eye, different to the content calmness of his family's horses.

"Hi," Andrew said from atop the mare.

James looked up and up to see his face. "Hi," James said in return. "I'm James. Nice horse."

Andrew patted the mare's neck. "Her name is CC."

"How tall is she?"

"About seventeen hands high. Careful. She bites." He laughed as CC snapped her teeth and James withdrew his hand from the fence just in time. "Are you visiting the property next door?"

"No, I live here now. Do you know Cassandra? She's my sister."

James watched Andrew's ears turn red and felt curious.

"Yes, I've met her. Listen, I've got to run. See ya!" Andrew turned CC and they galloped away.

It seemed to James that maybe Andrew liked Cassandra. He grinned to himself and went back to the house.

He found Cassandra at the dining table with Ray. She introduced him and James sat down to join in their afternoon tea of carrot cake. He noticed that Ray was infatuated with Cassandra. She seemed uncomfortable about something.

After a while, Ray left and Cassandra started cleaning. When she started the washing up, James picked up a black and white checked tea towel to dry the dishes. "Ray really likes you," he said.

Cassandra tensed.

Ray had come over today to ask her out and she had said no. He had become pushy, wanting her to come over to his place, but then James had shown up—thankfully—and Ray left. She had woken up to the fact that she was attracted to Ray for his incredibly good looks, but she really didn't want to go out with him. Ray had tried to open her up and talk about personal subjects, but she had refused.

She explained all this to James, surprised at how easy he was to talk to.

They finished cleaning and James wandered upstairs to his bedroom. He had started reading a series of books his mother was writing. He saw the book he was currently reading lying on top of the wooden chest.

He went to pick it up, then stopped. He knelt by the wooden chest and moved the book to the floor. Slowly he lifted the lid of the chest.

Inside were all his memories of his first four years spent at this house. He sifted through all sorts of things, including a packet of crayons, a wooden puzzle, drawings he and Cassandra had done, a toy dog, a racing car set, and a small fire engine truck.

At the bottom of the chest was an envelope. He picked it up and opened it to find a few photos. The photos had been taken outside the house.

One was of his father riding a grey horse streaking past the camera like lightning.

Another photo showed the same horse, standing still with four-year-old James smiling happily while sitting in the saddle.

Other photos showed Cassandra and his mother laughing and playing without a hint of sadness. But James felt sad looking at these photos. They were taken not long before the kidnapping.

"You can keep these photos for your very own, James," his mother had said, smiling at her infant son.

She watched as his face lit up and he ran upstairs straight away to secrete them in the chest.

He looked at a stick figure drawing he had done of his family. Cassandra's face had a big smile. He had drawn huge, black circles on his head to represent his curls. He had tried to draw a tie on his father and a pink dress on his mother. He remembered bits and pieces of his infanthood, each memory a happy one.

But four years was a short period of time and most of James's memories were wrapped up in the ten years following the kidnapping. Terror, pain, and worst of all, missing his family. It would take a long time for him to come to grips.

But he was strong. All the pain was in the past.

He was home with his family at last.

CHAPTER 13

Ray

The rest of the school holidays passed quickly for Cassandra. She continued teaching James piano, exercising Jet, helping with housework, and trying to avoid Ray. Ray was persistent. He left her no space, and because she often liked to be alone to be at peace, Cassandra's wall rebuilt itself, locking her heart.

In the last week of the holidays, Cassandra was out the front of her parents' house playing with the family cats when Ray approached her on foot. "Hi," he greeted her solemnly.

Cassandra looked up then slowly got to her feet.

"We need to talk, Cassandra, about us."

Cassandra had been expecting this moment. As the cats purred at her feet, she said simply, "I don't want a boyfriend right now."

There, she had said it.

Ray couldn't help the feelings he had for this girl, but he understood she wasn't ready to go out with him yet. He could not meet her eyes.

There was an uncomfortable silence between them.

"Well, maybe we can still be friends," Ray suggested.

Cassandra nodded, not knowing what to say.

"Maybe I'll see you round," Ray said then strode away.

Cassandra watched with a mixed feeling of relief and sadness coursing through her.

CHAPTER 14

School

The next week school began. James qualified for year 9. As he and Cassandra walked to school together the first day, James felt nervous despite his family's reassurances that everything would be fine. He had to wear a blue and grey uniform with a tie.

Cassandra wore a senior uniform for the first time, a white blouse and grey skirt. She felt perfectly happy to be returning to school as she did not mind learning and studying.

The high school was less than an hour's walk. Halfway there, they met up with Andrew. He was even more nervous than James about attending a new school because he had a shy streak. He wanted to be out riding CC instead.

Andrew said hi to them. He had spoken to James a few times in the holidays. Cassandra smiled at him and he walked on the other side of James so Cassandra wouldn't see his ears turn red. James took this in with a grin. Now that Cassandra wasn't seeing Ray anymore, Andrew had a chance.

As they walked, Cassandra filled them in with details of the high school.

"The principal, Mr Whitehall, is strict but fair. When you're in class, if the teacher writes your name on the blackboard, you're either in for detention or you're going to be sent to the principal's office. You can get into trouble easily, you know, talking in class, being late, spitballs, fighting, whatever."

James smiled at her enthusiasm. *Who likes school?* His stomach was in knots.

Andrew was happy to see Cassandra happy. He didn't mind school either, but he hadn't ever had to change schools before. His nervousness was starting to make him feel sick.

When the school came into view, Cassandra pointed out the red brick buildings and named them as the maths department, English, history, science, etc.

When they arrived, they had to line up for early morning assembly. Cassandra pointed James in the direction of the year 9 lines. Andrew was in year 11 with her. They lined up together facing the principal and schoolteachers.

At 8:45 a.m. the school bell rang loud and clear to signal the start of the school day. A school anthem began, and the kids had to sing along. Most didn't.

Mr Whitehall addressed them, welcoming them back to another year at Casyarna High. Timetables were handed out, then three new schoolteachers were introduced.

One of the teachers introduced was in her first teaching job. She was young with an hourglass figure. She was horrified when some of the boys started clapping and wolf whistling—too loudly for the principal's liking. Mr Whitehall silenced them by stating clearly, "Anyone who behaves like that in future in front of any teacher will answer to me."

He turned his back for a moment, and one of the students yelled out, "Why? *You want her for yourself?*"

Mr Whitehall whipped round, furious, but didn't know which kid had spoken. A sea of innocence looked up at him. The teachers kept straight faces.

He turned his back to signal the end of assembly.

Everyone started rushing around to get to their classes on time.

As it turned out, Andrew was in some of Cassandra's classes. He knew from Ray that Cassandra usually just wanted to be alone, so he didn't sit next to her in class. All that day, he felt he was in a dream, drifting from class to class trying not to get lost. During the lunch break, he was sitting alone when James appeared out of nowhere to sit with him. But after lunch, it was back to classes until 2:50 p.m. when at long last the bell rang to signal they could go home.

As Andrew walked out of his last class, James saw him and ran over, happy to recognise a face in the press of students eager to leave the school grounds.

"Walk home with us," James invited. "Cassandra said to meet her at the flagpole."

They met up with Cassandra. She felt comfortable in the presence of her brother and new friend. She chatted happily on the way home. Andrew listened to every word, walking beside her this time, quite taken with her beauty.

James only half listened, glad the day was over. He couldn't wait to get home.

CHAPTER 15

Shyness

In the first two weeks of school, James did well. He didn't like the timetables or being told what to do, but he threw himself into his studies and concentrated in class. He grew accustomed to the rules and made friends with two students, Brendan and Dave.

It was different for Andrew. He didn't mind the routines; he was punctual and bookish anyway. But he had that shy streak. When conversation was inevitable, he often surprised himself by being able to participate, especially with his sense of humour. But he didn't like attention being brought onto him, and when people were around, he was usually nervous. He didn't make true friends at Casyarna High, and he kept thinking of his old school and friends. But then there was Cassandra.

He wanted to go out with her but was too shy to ask. He was sure she would say no anyway. A girl that stunningly beautiful, who made boys' heads turn, could have any boy she wanted; surely she wouldn't want a shy boy like him. Cassandra had spirit, she liked challenges, and she always seemed to know what to say to people.

Her eyes. They fascinated him. They were a rainbow of colour; they even had aqua flecks. Who had ever seen eyes with aqua flecks before? His eyes were plain dark brown. He often wondered what people thought when he turned his eyes away because of shyness.

He was so caught up with being shy that Andrew didn't notice Cassandra's interest in him. She would notice him in their classes together. He was good-looking like his brother but so different. Ray was older and pushy. Andrew was her age and quiet. Ray had towered over her at over six feet high, but Andrew was only slightly taller than her. Andrew's hair was a much darker brown than Ray's.

Something about Andrew's shyness and sensitivity drew her to him, but Cassandra kept this to herself. She contented herself with schoolwork, not realising that Andrew could actually like such a stubborn, spoiled girl as herself!

James couldn't believe the two of them. It was obvious they should be together. Yet they hardly spoke to each other!

One day as they were walking home from school, James saw his friend Dave up ahead. "There is Dave," he said to Cassandra and Andrew. "I'll go say hi!" And with that, he jogged to catch up with Dave, leaving them alone.

Andrew was quiet. Cassandra asked him how CC was.

"She's fine," Andrew replied.

Cassandra wished she could spark some interest in Andrew; he was so quiet! Did he find her boring?

Andrew wished he weren't so nervous around her. It was a relief when they said goodbye out the front of his parents' house and he walked inside. From a front window, he watched Cassandra walk away up the road to her house.

When she was gone, he turned around, and there was Ray with pain in his eyes, reading him as though he were an open book, just like the older brother always had.

CHAPTER 16

Cassandra's Choice

Cassandra's birthday was in autumn. That year it was on a Saturday. She woke up feeling happy to be turning sweet sixteen. She jumped out of bed, had a quick shower, and then went for a walk in the crisp morning air. The trees were letting their leaves fall in splashes of red and gold. Cassandra shuffled through them until she heard her family start breakfast, then she headed back inside.

Valery was preparing golden pancakes with hot maple syrup. Everyone wished her a happy birthday.

Afterwards, her parents gave her a gold necklace with matching bracelet. Cassandra hugged her parents and put the jewellery on straight away.

James had used their father's camera that past week to take photos of Jet when his sister wasn't around to see. He gave her a framed photo of Jet cantering and free across the land, mane and tail flowing. It made Cassandra catch her breath it was so beautiful. She thanked her brother with delight.

James had discovered he liked photography and was about to say so when there was a knock on the door.

Cassandra and her parents sat in the lounge room as James answered the door. Andrew stood outside nervously, holding a dozen red roses. James invited him inside and showed him into the lounge room.

As soon as Andrew saw Cassandra, his ears turned red.

"Happy birthday," Andrew said, holding out the fragrant flowers.

Cassandra's face lit up. She stood gracefully to take the flowers from his hand, her fingers lightly brushing his.

"I'll go find a vase," Valery offered, giving Andrew a smile. She and John left the lounge room. James leaned up against the archway entrance of the lounge room, aware that Cassandra and Andrew were oblivious of him.

Andrew smiled at Cassandra. "James told me it was your birthday today. Do you like the flowers?"

Cassandra nodded. Her heart was beating terribly fast, and her fingers were tingling from touching his.

"I have another present for you," he said shyly.

Then, finally giving her direct eye contact, he gave her two movie tickets.

Cassandra looked up in surprise. She had wanted to see this movie, and to go with Andrew would be perfect!

"Thank you," she breathed.

There was another knock on the door. James opened it to see Ray trying to look in the front window at Andrew and Cassandra. James cleared his throat to get Ray's attention.

Ray whipped round and gave James a wide smile.

"I'm here to see Cassandra," he announced.

James let him in. He knew Ray had feelings for Cassandra, but then so did his younger brother. Now Cassandra had both Anderson brothers in front of her, and she had to choose.

James settled back in an armchair to watch.

Ray ignored Andrew and wished her a happy birthday. He gave her a single red silk rosebud and said that silk is forever.

Andrew stared at the floor.

Cassandra stood with silk in one hand and movie tickets in the other.

"Would you like to go horse riding today?" Ray asked her.

She watched as he brushed his fringe off his forehead and smiled. He was *gorgeous*. But she knew he wasn't the type of person she wanted to be with, so her eyes settled on Andrew. Andrew looked up in surprise as she ignored Ray, put down the silk rosebud, and stepped up to him.

"I'd love to spend the day with you," she said to Andrew.

Andrew's face lit up and then they were gone, the fake flower lying forgotten on top of a polished coffee table.

Ray stared after them then turned to see James looking at him sympathetically.

"She has made her choice," James said.

Ray turned and left.

CHAPTER 17

Family Reunion

The movie theatre was in town. Cassandra and Andrew decided to walk there.

In one scene of the movie, a young horse was injured and almost killed. Cassandra felt tears spring to her eyes. She couldn't bear the thought of anything like that happening to Jet.

She jumped slightly as she felt Andrew cover her hand lightly with his. She felt a thrill at his touch and suddenly realised this was the beginning of a relationship. She went hot all over.

Afterwards, they bought raspberry sodas to sip on the way home. Cassandra had always felt happy to be in Andrew's presence, so she talked freely to him. This allowed Andrew to be himself, quiet but happy to join in the conversation without force. Neither of them felt uncomfortable or nervous.

When they reached Cassandra's house, the two cats were playing together out front. Cassandra and Andrew sat on the grass in the early afternoon sunshine with an orange and white cat named Marmalade and a grey cat named Smokey.

After a while, Andrew caught Cassandra's hand. Standing, he slowly he drew her to her feet. His hands circled her waist and she stepped closer to him. Putting her arms around him, they kissed for the first time.

As their lips parted, Cassandra smiled and looked into Andrew's gorgeous, expressive, deep-brown eyes. Then they both stiffened as they heard a snigger behind them.

Turning around, they faced a group of people walking out of the house to watch them! Cassandra drew in her breath sharply—a surprise sweet sixteen birthday party with her whole family visiting and watching! As her cheeks reddened and Andrew's ears burned savagely, her family watched with amusement and called out "Surprise!" and "Happy birthday!"

Cassandra composed herself, grabbed Andrew's hand, and pulled him up to the house. She smiled at everyone: grandparents, her father's two older brothers and their families, her mother's younger sister, Andrew's family, and James's friends from school. Everyone moved into the house that was now decorated with purple, pink, and white balloons and streamers. Taking a deep breath, Cassandra turned around and said, "What a surprise! I would never have guessed! Thank you, all!"

"Open the presents!" one of her small cousins yelled, unable to keep his hands off them.

"Hey, check out the cake!" another cousin yelled from the kitchen.

As parents scolded and onlookers laughed, Valery ushered everyone out to the back garden, where several picnic tables were laden with all sorts of food. As people started eating, someone put on music and the party began.

The party wasn't only for Cassandra. It was also a chance for James to reunite with his family and meet some of them for the first time. Everyone approached him.

His father had two older brothers, both married with children. Uncle Daniel and his wife, Jackie, greeted him warmly and introduced him to their four children: Kelly, age nineteen, Aaron, seventeen, Amy ten, and Jack, four. The whole family was polite. Daniel was a strict father but was close to all four children. With Jackie, he had a happy marriage.

Uncle Mike and Aunty Kerryn were extroverts who were loud and cheerful with fun natures. They had James laughing with funny stories. They had two children: Christopher, seven, and Jenny, five. Kerryn pointed the two out to James just in time for him to see Christopher pull Jenny's hair. As Jenny poked her tongue out at her brother, Kerryn walked over to scold them and they ran off.

Valery's sister Michelle was thirty-one. She was sitting with her boyfriend, Matthew. They told James of their busy career lives and their ideas of living together. James smiled, wondering if they were thinking of marriage.

James liked both his mother's parents and his father's parents.

When Valery brought out the cake, they all sang happy birthday. Everyone agreed the cake was beautiful. It was shaped like a piano, with white icing and liquorice for the keys. When Cassandra cut into the cake, she found out it was her favourite kind, a jumble cake with swirls of vanilla and chocolate throughout its centre. Christopher, Jenny, and Jack all wanted seconds.

Afterwards, they all walked into the lounge room to watch Cassandra open the presents. She was given lots of lovely things, including clothing, jewellery, a diary, and a letter writing set. She loved every present and thanked everyone. When the last present was opened, people began to leave.

At the end of the party, there was a knock on the already open front door. Most of the guests had already left or were saying goodbye.

John walked to the door and smiled at the girl standing there.

"May I help you?" he asked.

"I'm here to pick up my brother Brendan Rosewell," she said.

John showed her through the house to the back garden. James, Brendan, Dave, Cassandra, and Andrew were outside talking and laughing as they cleared the picnic tables. John led the girl over to Brendan who said hi, and then John disappeared back inside the house.

"This is my sister Bridget," Brendan announced.

James was laughing at something silly Dave had said, but when he turned to meet Bridget, his mouth almost dropped open.

Bridget was pretty and slender. At seventeen, she was six feet tall with a wild tumble of red curls. She had green eyes with a cool, confident gaze that had direct eye contact—no shy petal this one. Car keys dangled from her left hand as the fingers on her right hand moved through her hair. She waited patiently for Brendan to say goodbye, then they left.

James found himself staring at the back door where she disappeared. He felt strange all over because of her. Her green eyes had skimmed over him, leaving him shaken.

Snap out of it, he thought.

He turned to speak to Cassandra about the cleaning up and found she was watching him.

As James turned to her, she and Andrew looked at each other and grinned.

CHAPTER 18

New Love

James was tortured with dreams about the redhead for the next few nights. In school he found himself listening closely to anything Brendan said about Bridget, without giving away his feelings for her.

Bridget was in year 12. James was only in year 9. Sometimes he would see her in the school grounds. She was always surrounded by friends and having a great time. She was so beautiful James ached to kiss her. He watched love blossom between his sister and Andrew as they grew more affectionate day by day.

He watched his parents enjoy their marriage and express their love in small ways such as leaving love notes for each other or John's eyes lighting as Valery melted in his arms. All James felt was emptiness.

When James had been taken from his family, he had felt great loss and homesickness. Now that he had returned home, the cure was as bad as the loss because it made him realise he needed more. He could never receive the type of love and happiness he craved from family. He actually wanted to start his own family.

All James could think about was Bridget. He lost interest in his classes. One clear autumn morning, he was in a history class, sitting up the back of the classroom and thinking about Bridget, when he suddenly heard his name.

"James! Are you just going to sit there or at least pretend to do some of the work like the rest of the class?"

James jumped and looked up at the history teacher, a strict, no-nonsense, middle-aged man with a thick moustache. James looked at the clock on the wall and realised he had just daydreamed through half of the lesson.

"Well?" Mr Lane asked impatiently.

James was about to reply, but Mr Lane cut him off with "I've seen you daydream once too often, young man. I expect to see you in lunchtime detention today, or a note goes home to your parents." Mr Lane lifted his eyebrows for emphasis.

James nodded and opened his textbook to read over the lesson. Making some notes in his exercise book seemed to satisfy Mr Lane, who then went back to the front of the classroom.

In his next lesson, maths, James caught up with Dave and told him about receiving detention.

"Good one," Dave laughed. "Looks like you've settled in just fine."

James arrived at the detention room a few minutes early. He slouched to the back of the room and sat down heavily. The top of the wooden desk was covered with small pictures, some carved and some in blue pen. He looked down at tiny skulls, snakes, and swords. He could feel the teacher's eyes everywhere in that small, cold room. His punishment was to write, "I will not daydream in class," repeatedly until the end of the lunch break in an hour's time. Sighing, he started.

Then Bridget walked in.

Mr Lane glowered at her.

"Well, it's you again. No surprise there! What is it this time?"

Bridget gazed straight at the history teacher.

"I've been caught talking in class. You will see me here all week."

Mr Lane sat back with his hands behind his head.

"No doubt you've been arguing with your maths teacher, back answering your English teacher, and who knows what else. Is talking in class your favourite pastime this year, or is it skipping classes like last year? How you've made it to year 12 is beyond me."

Bridget didn't reply. Turning around, she headed straight to the back of the room and slid gracefully behind a desk beside James. James's stomach was suddenly full of butterflies.

A few other kids filed into the room not looking impressed at having to be there, but James's spirits had lifted upon seeing Bridget. He was imagining ways of talking to her when a small, balled-up piece of paper landed on the desk in front of him. He almost dropped his pen in surprise. He glanced up to make sure Mr Lane was looking elsewhere before reading the note.

> Hi, aren't you my brother's friend? I haven't seen you in detention before. Congrats if this is your first time. This is so boring! I wish Mr Lane would drop out the window, then we could get out of here!

James kept a straight face. He wrote back,

> Yes, I'm Brendan's friend. Mr Lane is so fat he would probably just bounce back in. James

Bridget laughed out loud when she read what he wrote. This of course got the teacher's attention.

Mr Lane stormed over and roared that both Bridget and James were now on two weeks' detention. He picked up the note but didn't read it. He crumpled it up and threw it on his desk.

"I'll save it for later," he said stonily.

Bridget was as calm as ever. James was worried what punishment Mr Lane would deal out to them when he read that note.

He needn't have worried.

One of the kids up the front of the room sitting right next to Mr Lane's desk grabbed the note when Mr Lane wasn't looking and replaced it with a blank piece of paper. The note itself made its way back to Bridget without Mr Lane noticing.

At the end of the hour, Bridget wrote on the note.

> That was a close one. See you tomorrow in detention.
> Bridget

James clutched the note and smiled at her.
She smiled back.

CHAPTER 19

What to Wear!

Later that week, Bridget approached Brendan, Dave, and James after school one day. Brendan grinned at her. "Hi, sis," he greeted.

Bridget smiled at him.

"There's going to be a grunge party this weekend and you're all invited," she said simply. "It's going to be on Saturday night by Cliff Edge." She looked at each of them in turn, her gaze lingering on James's face.

As she turned and left, he felt the ache to kiss her.

The three friends turned and started walking home. Dave and Brendan filled James in on what a grunge party was.

"There will be great rock music and you wear grunge clothes. It'll be by the river where it's deep enough to jump off the cliff edge," Brendan explained.

"It'll go all night. Don't expect to get any sleep. After all, there will be girls there." Dave grinned. Girls were all Dave thought about, and he was open about it.

Cassandra and Andrew walked close together. They had heard about the party and knew it was for anyone who felt like showing up. Neither was fussed with the idea of going, but Andrew wanted to see what happened at a party like that. They knew Bridget had planned the party with her friends.

Bridget was popular. She had a reputation of going out of her way to help people, plus she had a fun personality, but she was always in detention for talking in class or for not showing up for class and Cassandra had always avoided her.

Andrew was in the process of winning Cassandra over to the idea of going to the party by whispering sweet nothings in her ear. He told her about things they could get up to on a beautiful night in autumn by a moonlit river, delighting in Cassandra's smiles and blushes.

Needless to say, he won.

Valery and John reluctantly agreed to letting their teenage children go to the party but gave them a curfew of midnight. Cassandra didn't mind the curfew, but James didn't like it. However, he didn't argue with his father's "Don't mess with me" look or his mother's worry.

On the evening of the party, Cassandra was thrown into a girlish fit over what to wear. A grunge party meant daggy clothes.

James had simply opened his bag from the orphanage. In it, he had faded, tattered jeans, an old black T-shirt, and a flannelette shirt that had a long rip down one sleeve. Since arriving home, he had been wearing new clothes of fine cotton or wool. Clothes that fitted him well provided for him by his parents. Somehow wearing his old daggy clothes made him feel comfortable whereas he always used to be embarrassed by them. But he knew everyone would be dressed like this tonight.

He was in the lounge room when Cassandra walked in wearing decent clothes, thinking she was dressed in grunge. James laughed and pointed out that her jeans were new. She tried on another outfit in useless anger and then changed clothes again. She was feeling exasperated when Andrew arrived.

John let Andrew in and joked, "Careful, Andrew. With her temper, you could get burned."

By this time, Cassandra was now wearing old sneakers, a pair of jeans only slightly faded, and one of her father's old woolly jumpers. She felt a mess. Her hair hung in long tangles from pulling clothes on and off.

Andrew picked up most of this just from looking at her. In front of her family, he took her hand. "You're beautiful, and I love you," he said.

Everyone could see the sincerity in his eyes.

Cassandra blushed, relaxing back into happiness.

Her parents smiled, enjoying the calming influence Andrew had on their daughter. They had talked at length about Cassandra and this first boyfriend and agreed he was right for her.

They were finally ready to head off to the party.

CHAPTER 20

The Grunge Party

They set off on horseback later that evening. James didn't know how to ride a horse very well, but he had had a few lessons from his father. He rode Des. The old grey was good with beginners. Andrew rode his mother's black gelding knowing that CC was likely to play up, and Cassandra rode Jet, "her other man" as Valery had jokingly put it earlier in the evening.

There were two full moons glowing that autumn night. They took it easy on the way to the river, James conscious of his clumsy riding and Cassandra and Andrew looking as though they were born on horseback.

It wasn't long before they heard music pumping. They urged their horses along the river to a large outcropping of rock known as Cliff Edge, where teenagers were sitting. By the riverbank were more people, and not far from them was a picket line for horses. Andrew led the way. They made sure their horses were settled, and then James saw Bridget. When Cassandra and Andrew looked up from their horses, James had disappeared.

Bridget arrived on a galloping albino horse, its white coat almost glowing in the moonlight. The horse came to a sliding standstill in the middle of a group of her friends. Some of them cursed in surprise and dropped things. Bridget laughed. She apologised for the scare, smiling as friends greeted her. She slid off the albino to lead him to the picket line when she noticed James standing alone. He stood casually, one hand in a pocket, giving her direct eye contact.

Bridget stared at him and swallowed hard. In school, he looked somewhat young and innocent. Right now, his intense gaze went straight through her, making her feel vulnerable, making him appear so much older.

She took in his sharp face, lean body, and strong arms. He was tall and confident, and she suddenly found it hard to believe he was younger than she was.

James stood calmly, but he felt nervous.

There she was. Pale skin with shoulder-length red curls, tall, slender, and beautiful. He walked towards her and said, "Good evening."

Bridget smiled and suddenly melted. She took a step towards this all-knowing boy, and they embraced.

They kissed passionately, feeling a kind of connection and fondness neither understood.

They tied the albino with the other horses. James patted the strong white shoulder. "Is he your horse?" he asked.

Bridget laughed. "I wish," she replied. "His name is Lightning; he belongs to a friend." Sighing, she explained how she had always wanted a horse but there was no way her parents could have one.

"Lucky you're so popular." James grinned. Most of the students at Casyarna High had horses.

Bridget feigned surprise. "Popular? Me?" she wondered aloud.

James laughed and took her in his arms. "You know you are," he said.

Bridget hugged him, and then they walked hand in hand to the riverbank to easily mingle with the large crowd.

Cassandra and Andrew were in their own world. They had found a moonlit patch of grass not far from the horses. Over the past weeks, their love had deepened. They sat close together, sharing each other's feelings.

Andrew told Cassandra he loved her again and then stood drawing her up with him. Cassandra could see the truth in his eyes. The wall around her heart crumbled completely as they kissed passionately.

James saw their closeness and smiled, happy for his sister. As he stood watching, Bridget sidled up to him.

"Care for a hug?" she asked, playfully running her fingers through his black hair.

James embraced her from behind so they could both watch his sister.

Bridget leaned back against him. "Isn't that your sister?" she asked in surprise. "And the new kid, the one who can barely talk?"

She watched them kiss again then added, "My, my, maybe Cassandra has a heart after all."

James stiffened. "What's that supposed to mean?" he asked quite fiercely.

Bridget jumped at the protectiveness in his voice. She blushed.

"Nothing. I didn't mean that the way it sounded. It's just that Cassandra has always been alone in school; no one could get close to her. She is good at giving the cold shoulder."

Bridget was quiet for a moment then said, "Maybe she has changed."

James thought about what Bridget said and relaxed his stiffened grip.

Bridget turned to face him, running her hands up his arms as she did so. She felt the scar, glanced down curiously, but decided not to say anything as James's lips met hers in a fulfilling kiss.

The rest of the night passed quickly. Some of the boys sitting on Cliff Edge became tipsy and leapt off the rock into the river for fun. When they climbed out of the cold water into the cool air, they regretted the sobering leap and were harassed by friends. One of them was Dave. He saw James laughing at him and grinned back sheepishly. Everyone had a great time. They all enjoyed the heavy music played on someone's stereo.

When it came time to go home, James didn't want to leave Bridget. Bridget didn't want to be without him, her new love, so she rode with him.

CHAPTER 21

The Outcome

The ride home was fun for the four of them. James was a clumsy rider. Bridget picked on him about it, but she was so funny he just laughed at her teasing. Cassandra and Andrew watched the new couple, happy for them.

They arrived back at James's parents' property shortly before midnight. Cassandra and Andrew said their goodbyes and then Andrew continued on his way home. Bridget and James helped Cassandra settle Jet, Des, and Lightning before going into the house. Cassandra was tired. She said goodnight and went straight to bed.

This left James and Bridget alone together in the lounge room. Bridget walked around the beautiful room as if in a dream, exclaiming in delight at vases, statues, photos, and furniture. James sat in an armchair watching and smiling.

After a while, Bridget stopped talking. She stepped towards James slowly across an oriental rug. A lamp shed a soft glow over the two of them as he sunk into the chair, pulling her onto his lap. As he cupped her breast with his hand and she gently kissed him, they both realised this wasn't the first time for either of them. Quickly he picked her up and carried her up the stairs to his bedroom.

Their lovemaking was easy. James was a passionate considerate person. Bridget was bold and loving. Both had confidence to satisfy the other.

Afterwards they lay tangled in each other's arms.

When James fell asleep, Bridget slipped out of his bed, down the stairs, and outside to where Lightning was waiting patiently. She patted the fine animal, mounted, and urged him towards home.

CHAPTER 22

The Andersons

The next morning, James felt lonely in his bed by himself. He understood that Bridget would have wanted to return Lightning to his rightful owner and arrive home safe by morning. He was grateful she had slipped away in the night because he was sure his mother wouldn't appreciate finding him in bed with a girl. He concentrated on playing the piano that day. His parents were busy as usual, and his sister headed straight over to Andrew's house after breakfast.

Cassandra was welcome at the Anderson house anytime. She wanted to see Andrew's baby photos and asked Gabrielle if this was OK. Gabrielle was delighted and went to get the photo albums.

"You're such a *girl*," Andrew teased Cassandra.

They waited in the lounge room with Jess and Alex until Gabrielle returned with the albums, six to be exact. Andrew wasn't keen on the sight of so many, but Cassandra's face lit up.

The first album had a cream cover and contained Gabrielle and Bryan's wedding photos. Gabrielle's wedding dress had white lace puffy sleeves, and her flowers were yellow and white roses. Cassandra was surprised to see baby Raymond in the bride's arms. Gabrielle explained how she knew Bryan would be her husband before they were engaged, then while they were engaged, she had fallen pregnant with Raymond.

"We didn't have enough money for a big wedding. The reception was for family and a few close friends. My aunty made the dress, and my mother grew the flowers. A friend took the photos, but I think Raymond got the most attention!" She laughed.

The next album had a flower pattern on the cover and contained early childhood photos of Ray and Andrew with their parents. Andrew looked no different, except his hair was a lighter brown in his primary school photos and he didn't start wearing glasses until high school;

however, it was a surprise to see that Ray was a rather chubby child. The photos were of them playing cricket or football, first days in school, and their birthdays. The first house they lived in looked small and plain but nice on the inside, with one paddock out the back.

"We worked hard to be able to move up here," Gabrielle remembered. "Bryan sometimes worked two jobs. It wasn't until he left one job after a long time and got a huge payout that we could afford a deposit on this house. His parents are paying for Raymond's education at the university."

Jess and Alex stayed quiet, content to look at each photo album after Gabrielle was finished showing them to Cassandra and Andrew. They sat on the floor in front of a window seat their mother shared with Cassandra and Andrew.

The third album was yellow. This had the baby photos. Andrew had been a shy baby. Raymond had been chubby and cheerful. Jess and Alex were adorable identical babies who had attracted a lot of attention, even by people in the street. Gabrielle was happy to explain certain photos.

"Raymond won a beautiful baby contest," she said, pointing out the winning photo. It showed Ray in a bubble bath holding up a toy yellow duck to the camera with a cheeky smile.

"This is Andrew's first step, heading straight for a horse of course!" This showed an eleven-month-old Andrew heading for his father, who was holding out a soft brown and white toy horse.

There was a photo of Jess and Alex in a pink twin stroller that had white wheels and a small pink and white umbrella attached to keep the sun out of their eyes. In the photo, both girls were wearing pink sunglasses and looking straight at the camera with big cheeky grins.

"That's my favourite photo," Jess told Cassandra.

Next, Gabrielle picked up an album that had a picture of three white puppies playing in spring grass on the cover. This consisted of grandparent photos. Cassandra could see Andrew's eyes were the same as Bryan's father's, deep brown. There were also photos of Reg, Petey, and Cinderella, the horses, and Gabrielle's canary, Sunshine.

There was one photo of Andrew standing beside CC in the paddock of the first house. He was about thirteen. CC had her ears back and was in sorry condition, rough coated with ribs showing through.

"Andrew saved CC from cruelty and saved her life," Gabrielle said proudly.

The last two photo albums showed photos of birthdays, Christmases, and family get-togethers. When they finished looking through them, Andrew was relieved. Six albums of photos he had already seen before was a bit much! But he had liked watching Cassandra enjoy them.

Putting the albums down, Gabrielle requested she speak to Cassandra in private and asked Andrew to take the twins outside for a riding lesson. Andrew felt a bit put out. The twins became clamorous when he hesitated because they loved horse riding. They dragged him outside joyfully.

Gabrielle half turned on the window seat to face Cassandra. "Bryan and I want you to know we are very happy for you and Andrew," she began. "We've both seen how Andrew comes out of his shell when you're around; he is so much happier. The love you both share is obvious at first glance." Gabrielle took one of Cassandra's hands.

Cassandra looked up to meet Gabrielle's warm, motherly gaze.

"Cassandra, I want you to talk to Raymond. I know you've been wrapped up in Andrew lately. I think maybe you've forgotten Ray's feelings for you. Both my sons have always been sensitive to rejection. Since your birthday, Raymond has been so sad, although we can see he has accepted your choice of boyfriend. Please talk to him. There is tension between him and his brother that has never been there before. Maybe you can help with that."

Nodding, Cassandra felt guilty. What Gabrielle had said was true; she had been too wrapped up in Andrew to remember she had hurt Ray.

"I'm sorry," she whispered.

Gabrielle smiled. "Don't be sorry. I remember what it's like to be sixteen and in love. You're not guilty of anything. Please go speak to Ray. He is in the sunroom."

Gabrielle settled back on the window seat to look through one of the photo albums again while Cassandra made her way to the sunroom.

CHAPTER 23

Cassandra's Choice Accepted

Ray was sitting down at a table covered in pens, paper, and textbooks, frowning over his veterinary studies. He glanced up in surprise when Cassandra stopped to stand beside the table, looking uncertain about something. He closed the books, piling them in a neat stack. Cassandra sat in a chair opposite him, not sure what to say.

She looked at his good-looking face and took a deep breath. "Ray, I'm sorry because—"

Cassandra was lost for words. She blushed and tried again. "Ray, I know I've hurt you. Since I've started seeing your brother—" Her voice trailed off. Ray's blue eyes had her mesmerised. She wished she had thought of what she was going to say to this young man who she had once felt attracted to. She could see his feelings for her by the pain in his eyes. She wanted to run from him like she used to, but couldn't.

"I love Andrew," she finally stated. "We can still be friends, if you want to. I don't want to be the cause of any problems between you and your brother. I—"

"I know," Ray cut in. "You don't need to apologise for anything. Of course, we can still be friends. I can see that Andrew loves you."

Her choice of boyfriend seemed to be accepted. She smiled and took a deep breath. "How are things at uni?" she asked politely.

"Never studied so much in all my life!" Ray grinned. "But everything's fine."

They talked for a while about their studies, and then Ray asked her if she would like a shandy. Cassandra looked embarrassed as they both remembered the time she got tipsy in front of his parents. She asked for a glass of water.

Ray went into the kitchen and came back with glasses of water for both of them. He drank his in one long swallow. Cassandra stared at him. It was a big glass! Ray just shrugged and said he had been thirsty.

Then he saw that mischievous look in her eyes. He leaned forward eagerly and watched as Cassandra attempted to drink her water in one swallow. Halfway through, she started to laugh and then almost choked. Then they were both laughing.

Andrew gave his sisters their riding lesson. Their black and white ponies behaved, and his sisters rode well. Jess was talkative and adventurous. She longed for the day when she could own a large Thoroughbred and gallop freely across the hills. Alex had a growing interest in dressage and was reading a book on the subject.

Andrew liked to spend time with his sisters, but throughout the lesson all he could of was Cassandra.

After the lesson, Jess and Alex went inside to wash their hands and have lunch with their mother. Andrew walked into the sunroom to find his brother and girlfriend talking and laughing together. He wondered about them and thought of how sad Ray had been lately.

Ray looked at Andrew with a relaxed happy smile. Andrew could feel the tension lifting between them.

He went over to Cassandra, who reached out a hand to him. Andrew's features melted into love for her. He took a step forward then glanced back at Ray, who gave an "I understand" smile.

Andrew felt happy and knelt in front of Cassandra to hold her in his arms.

PART 2

BRIDGET SKY ROSEWELL

CHAPTER 24

A Request

The next few weeks passed pleasantly for the families. Cassandra and Andrew were as close as ever, although they remained shy regarding further intimacy. They liked to take things slow, think about the consequences of actions, and make plans for the future.

It was different for James and Bridget. They took great pleasure in making love and thoroughly enjoyed each other's company. They were always having fun. Somehow they managed to keep their lovemaking a secret from their parents.

Winter began and the weather cooled dramatically. People started wearing woollen jumpers and gloves. Snow appeared on the Casyarna Mountains, but it never snowed as far down as Cassandra's parents' property.

One bright Friday, James and Bridget were walking together through the school football oval in their lunch break. James was thinking about how he had never seen Bridget's home and asked her about it.

She shrugged. "It's busy," she replied.

"How many are in your family?"

"I'm the eldest of eight. Let's see. There is Thomas, he's one, Melinda three, Sean five, Patrick eight, Christian ten, Holly twelve, and of course Brendan, fourteen. That's everyone."

"Eight! I'd like to meet this mob. How about I come over tomorrow?"

Bridget stopped walking. She looked worried about something. James asked what was wrong, but she just shook her head and hid her face from him for a moment. James took her hand.

Bridge had a decision to make. She had been thinking about whether James should meet her family or not for a while. To her, it was a difficult decision to make.

She gave a cool, unreadable smile.

"Sure, you can come over tomorrow. After all, you're my boyfriend and I love you. You should meet my family. Bring Cassandra and Andrew with you."

James took a step back, away from her green eyes. He thought he had seen them *change colour* slightly. He had stared into their depths and felt dizzy.

He was surprised at her request to bring Cassandra and Andrew with him, but just then, she'd appeared different, and that worried him. He felt sure he knew her. He knew he would appreciate his sister's—*anyone's*—company tomorrow.

CHAPTER 25

Was That a *Unicorn?*

At first Cassandra didn't want to go. She didn't understand why James would want his sister at his girlfriend's house. James didn't quite know either, and he certainly didn't know why Bridget requested Cassandra be there. He simply told Cassandra he would like her to become a friend of Bridget's. Andrew was happy to go, if only for the horse ride. Even CC put her ears forward and didn't seem so snappy.

Bridget arrived at James's parents' property early in the morning while riding Lightning bareback, to escort them to her place, the Rosewell home. James saddled Des. Cassandra, who had just exercised Jet, saddled her mother's palomino mare Golden Dream. Valery was busy working and had asked Cassandra to exercise Golden for her. They set off down the road, Cassandra and Andrew side by side behind James and Bridget.

Bridget got the four of them talking and laughing in the winter sunshine. The mountains were snowy, and the air was crisp. Everything was familiar. They were relaxed and having a great time, not paying much attention to their surroundings.

But suddenly they realised everything looked a lot different.

Cassandra stared around her with disbelieving eyes. The countryside was spring green and the Casyarna Mountains *weren't there* anymore. And was that a *unicorn* she saw cantering between trees over to their right? She pulled Golden to a stop, closed her eyes briefly, and opened them again only to find this was real. Her face went white. She thought about her mother's science fiction books. They couldn't be real, could they?

James and Andrew had also stopped their horses to take in their new surroundings.

Bridget turned her horse to face theirs. "Welcome to our world. Please don't be afraid. I know all this is strange to you. We'll take our time so you can get used to this place."

"Where exactly are we?" James asked.

"We're in the Centre World," Bridget replied.

"What? Where?" Andrew asked.

Bridget shrugged. "Centre World, World of Three Moons, World of the Gods. Where creatures from your world both mythical and extinct coexist. Where Cassandra and Andrew will realise their power. Where—"

"Enough!" Cassandra cried, shaking now. She didn't understand anything Bridget was saying.

Andrew dismounted. Stepping over to Golden, he pulled his girlfriend off the palomino to hold her in his arms. He refused to get upset.

James was curious. He was also amused. World of the Gods? He couldn't help slipping in a smart comment. "So is your middle name Heaven?" he asked.

Bridget stared at him. "No, it's Sky," she said seriously.

James grinned affectionately at her.

"Can you grow wings like an Angel and fly?" he asked cheekily.

Bridget was about to reply when they heard a great swooping noise above their heads. A shadow falling over them caused them all to look up as one.

There flew a magnificent white horse, its beautiful, feathered wings flapping lazily.

James's mouth dropped open, much to Bridget's satisfaction.

The horse flew off into the distance.

There was a moment of silence, and then Cassandra asked if this was a joke or not.

"Look into my eyes," Bridget demanded.

As they all complied, she stated, "No."

Turning Lightning around, she touched the albino to a canter. Cassandra and Andrew mounted and followed Bridget along with James.

Bridget stopped Lightning outside a large house. Everyone dismounted. The house stood in a valley, lonely and dejected. The horses were left tied to a fence with some water and hay before Bridget led her friends into the house. The interior was dark and shabby. The carpet had stains mixed in with its ratty brown colour. The whole place was damp and smelly. Bridget showed them through to the lounge room, and there was Brendan teaching his little sister Melinda to count. He jumped up in surprise when he saw who was with Bridget. He sent Melinda out to find his parents. Cassandra, James, and Andrew stood together in one corner, feeling awkward.

"Excuse us," he said politely, then he pulled Bridget into the kitchen.

"What can they see?" he whispered worriedly.

"Calm down, brother. They can only see the poor illusion," Bridget answered.

"And what is James doing here? You know he's not—"

"A God? No, but I'm in love with him," Bridget said fiercely, her hand moving to her belly. She looked deep into her brother's eyes. "It's time they learned who they are. Mum and Dad will be here any second. Go or stay. It's up to you."

Brendan stared at her, and then he noticed her hand on her belly. "You're not with child, are you? Mum and Dad will have kittens if—"

Bridget silenced him by shoving him back into the lounge room.

Everyone stood still in an uncomfortable silence, and then, with no warning, a man and a woman appeared out of thin air.

CHAPTER 26

Heaven

Bridget's parents stood side by side to regard the group of teenagers before them. Miranda was slender with red curls the same as Bridget, and Gavin was plump with grey hair. When their three-year-old daughter Melinda had summoned them, she had been crying that there was a mortal in Centre World.

Bridget's parents had known immediately it would have something to do with either Bridget or Brendan. Those two were usually quick to step out of line.

They saw Cassandra's frightened white face and smiled warmly at her. Andrew stood close to his girlfriend to lend comfort to her, both parents smiling at him approvingly. Then they turned their eyes on James. They saw a slightly nervous yet self-assured teenager who was obviously intelligent with depth.

James looked back at them. They were dressed poorly. He was wondering what was going on. Surely the House of Gods wouldn't be poor.

"No, we're not poor, James," Miranda said aloud.

James stared at her. He hadn't spoken!

Bridget cleared her throat nervously. "They can read minds," she explained apologetically.

Gavin faced his eldest daughter. "You have brought a mortal to Centre World," he snapped. "Just what do you have to say for yourself?"

Bridget stood up straight and tall. Looking her father straight in the eye, she said clearly, "I am in love with James and wish to bear his child."

There was a long, shocked silence.

Finally, James grabbed Bridget in a bear hug, their happiness and love apparent to all.

Gavin turned to Miranda. "What will we do with her?" he asked grouchily.

Miranda shrugged in the same manner adopted by her eldest daughter.

"Let them see our home," Bridget whispered. "Please let me lift this illusion. The time has come for Cassandra and Andrew, and James. Well, he might have to become a part of Centre World too. Let them know our names and begin learning today."

Her parents agreed reluctantly. They knew James was a passionate, honest person who wouldn't willingly harm anything. They nodded to Bridget, who then swept her left arm down in an arc, and their surroundings changed again.

They were above Centre World in between the clouds and outer space. Untouchable blue sky was all around. They walked on soft white *ground,* and sunrays shone through softly. Angels with beautiful wings played harps. The rest of the Rosewell family was there, looking at James curiously.

Miranda addressed Cassandra. "Tell me your middle name."

"Rainbow," Cassandra answered. She knew her mother had seen a glorious rainbow outside the hospital window when she was born.

"You are Cassandra Rainbow, God of rainbows."

While Cassandra pondered this, Miranda asked Andrew his middle name.

"Rain," Andrew replied.

"You are Andrew Rain, God of rain. You two are a match made in Heaven. Your middle names are joined. In other words, you can't have a rainbow without rain."

The young couple glanced at each other, finding all this confusing and hard to believe.

James stood with Bridget, hugging her from behind. They faced Miranda, who said, "Well, Bridget, you are in love with a mortal—"

"His name is James," Bridget interrupted.

Miranda smiled and addressed James. "You shouldn't be here now. You're not a God. But under the circumstances, all I can say is—"

Her voice trailed off and she glanced at Gavin. Bridget held her breath.

"All I can say is welcome." Miranda sighed.

CHAPTER 27

"Why Us?"

Bridget led James to her brothers and sisters to make introductions. Miranda and Gavin sat with Cassandra and Andrew to talk.

"What are your middle names?" Andrew asked.

Miranda answered. "Mine is Daylight, and Gavin's is Night."

"So you're the Gods of Day and Night," Cassandra said thoughtfully.

Miranda smiled. "That's right. We are the parents of Bridget Sky, Brendan River, Holly Flora, Christian Season, Patrick Leaf, Sean Cloud, Melinda Snowfall, and Thomas Mineral. All Gods. We are not the only God family here though."

"You will both come to realise that you are both Gods as well," Gavin said.

"Why us?" Cassandra asked.

Miranda answered, "Both you and your families believe in us. Both of you have the understanding and intelligence to be Gods. We knew you would fall in love and be able to have children. A decision awaits you. Do you want to remain mortals or be Gods? You actually get to decide, but you must have children—" Miranda's voice trailed off, and she turned her face away.

"We cannot have any more children ourselves," Gavin explained Miranda's obvious distress. "But more Gods are needed by the Rosewell family, which is why we've been choosing suitable Gods such as yourselves. There is another world Earth, known as World of One Moon, where three more Gods have been chosen. One girl has visited here and is in love with Brendan. Her name is Kayla Ocean, and she has decided to be a God. The other two are boys, and we are still waiting on their decisions."

Miranda faced them again. "If you decide to be mortal, you will still need to have children. Their middle names are already chosen. We know you are both in love; you're a match made in Heaven! From now on, you will be visiting Heaven regularly. We will meet again soon."

Then, with no warning, Miranda and Gavin vanished.

CHAPTER 28

Goodbye

Cassandra and Andrew clung to each other. Bridget saw her parents disappear and led James over to the confused, worried couple.

"Relax. You both have a couple of years to decide. Come on. Look at this place! Aren't you excited? You have powers!"

Cassandra's face went blank.

Andrew just stared at the redhead.

Bridget sighed. "Aren't you even curious?"

"What type of power are you talking about?" Andrew asked.

Bridget glanced around uncertainly for a moment, and then she swept her arm down again.

Jet appeared out of nowhere, swinging his head with annoyance. Cassandra and Andrew jumped, eyes wide.

"How did you do that?" Andrew asked.

Bridget laughed. "It's easy. You will learn."

Andrew swept his arm down, but nothing happened.

Bridget told him to picture in his mind what he wanted and to keep his eyes closed.

"Remember you're a God so this will work. Concentrate."

Andrew did as she said, murmuring, "CC," over and over. But when he opened his eyes, his face went white; he must have done something wrong! Instead of his chestnut mare, an exquisite woman with long, red hair almost to her feet stood before him.

"I'm sorry. I—I don't know who this is! I was trying to get my horse up here—"

Bridget cut him off, laughing. "You don't recognise the one you saved from cruelty?" she asked.

Andrew looked at the woman. He noticed her hair was the same colour as CC's. Her eyes were large and dark brown without any whites, like a horse! Was this CC?

"Can she talk?" Andrew asked Bridget.

"Of course I can talk!" the woman snapped angrily.

Andrew stepped back hastily.

"You're always so quick-tempered," Bridget said as she smiled at the woman.

CC stamped her foot before saying, "Well, in my previous life, I didn't have to suffer, and then bam! I die and you use me to be abused. And for what? You tell me!"

Bridget sighed. "That wasn't my decision. It was my parents'. You were cruel in your past life as a human. You treated horses terribly, even starved one while you lived a happy life! You needed to know what these defenceless horses went through. Besides, Andrew has treated you perfectly. Quit complaining."

CC softened a little. "I would like to thank you, Andrew, for looking after me so well."

She turned her face away before finishing with "I have learned a lesson."

With that, she walked away.

Bridget shook her head sadly. "Poor CC."

Andrew's face was still white. He had loved that mare and now he realised she wasn't his anymore. He felt Cassandra slip her hand into his. They watched the woman walk away until she disappeared.

"That's probably the closest you'll get to a goodbye," Bridget said softly to Andrew.

CHAPTER 29

To Sit and Talk

Early in the evening, they arrived back at Cassandra's parents' property through Bridget's magic. CC was not with them; she was to remain in Heaven. Andrew missed CC already.

They settled the horses before walking into the house. Valery was cooking, and the delicious smell of a casserole with hot bread rolls reminded the group how hungry they were. Valery invited Bridget and Andrew to stay for dinner. They accepted.

There was a while before dinner was ready. James led Bridget out to the front steps to sit and talk.

"So you wish to bear our child," James said softly, holding her close as they sat on the steps.

Bridget actually blushed. She shook her curls over her face in an attempt to hide it from him. When her face went back to normal colour, she looked directly at him.

"Your child is within me; I love you, and I know this baby is wanted by both of us."

James was so much in love with her he couldn't deny her words. He told her he loved her and couldn't wait to be a father.

Bridget placed his hand over her belly. Her hand remained on top of his, and they kissed under a starry night sky.

Cassandra and Andrew were in the lounge room snuggled together on an armchair. Cassandra rested her head on Andrew's chest.

"I find it all so hard to believe," she said.

"We need to believe. We have a lot of thinking ahead of us," Andrew responded.

"But *Gods?* What are we going to do when the choice is upon us? What—"

Andrew silenced her by gently placing a finger upon her lips. "We will work it out, Cassandra. We will have finished school by the time we have to make the decision."

He smiled lovingly at her. "We will do this together—maybe forever."

He watched as realisation dawned on Cassandra. They were immortal! They were in love, a match made in Heaven, love forever.

Happiness filled them both.

Rainbows—tiny, colourful, perfect arcs—appeared in Cassandra's eyes just before they kissed.

They had dinner that night with Bridget leading the conversation. She kept her pregnancy a secret from John and Valery, thinking maybe James should be the one to tell them at a suitable time. After eating, John went upstairs to read while Valery herded the teenagers into the kitchen to wash the dishes. Cassandra and Andrew obliged but Valery chased James and Bridget outside when they wouldn't stop flicking tea towels at each other.

Once outside, Bridget suddenly pulled a face. "I have to go. That was my father," she said, sighing.

James glanced around; Gavin was nowhere in sight. "What?"

Bridget smiled. "We can speak to each other with our minds," she explained, leaning up against him.

They said goodbye. She swept her arm down in an arc and then vanished.

James went back into the house.

Valery saw him. "Where's Bridget?" she asked.

"She had to leave," James answered.

"Will she arrive home safe?" motherly concern showed on Valery's face.

"Uh, sure. She knows the way. It's not too far. Goodnight!" James didn't really know what to say about Bridget's disappearance! He raced up the stairs to his bedroom.

Valery watched in surprise. He was going to bed? It was still early!

CHAPTER 30

The Replacement

When Andrew arrived back at his parents' house, he slowly climbed the stairs while thinking about CC. He met his sisters walking down the stairs towards him.

"Hi," Jessica greeted him. "How did CC go today?" She liked to ask Andrew about CC's progress in movement and temperament.

Andrew didn't know what to say. "Umm."

Gabrielle appeared to prepare the twins for bed and saved him from answering.

Andrew turned around and left the house. He went to the stables while wondering how he should explain CC's disappearance to people. He entered the stable, walked straight to CC's stall, and opened the stall door into an emptiness he felt within himself as much as the stall interior. Standing silently in the dark, Andrew remembered the first time he had seen CC.

He was thirteen and loved horses. His friend Steve owned a horse and taught Andrew how to ride.

Andrew's parents couldn't afford a horse back then, but there was a paddock out the back of the house, and when they first saw CC, they let Andrew look after her.

CC was abused by a drunken man. He bought her for his son who wasn't that keen on horses anyway. The son was lazy; he couldn't be bothered grooming her too often and sometimes forgot to feed her. The man was trying to become a good father. He had started drinking heavily when his wife had passed away. He was trying to give up the drinking and was ill-tempered and violent; he used to beat CC with a stick.

One evening the son left the gate to CC's paddock open. CC stumbled out onto the road and headed away from the hateful place that had harmed her spirit. She walked for a long time before stopping outside the Anderson place. A truck came tearing round the corner and frightened her. She reared and plunged to get out of the way, ending up in the middle of the Andersons' front yard. The truck went off into the distance without stopping.

Andrew befriended CC over time, and eventually he earned her trust.

Andrew took a deep breath. He had to get out of this stall and accept the fact she was gone. He turned around, took a step forward, and almost walked into—

Andrew blinked. In front of him stood a mare that looked exactly like CC yet wasn't CC. This mare pointed her ears forward and placed her muzzle into his hand. She shook her long chestnut mane, neighed, and looked past Andrew into the stall. Andrew laughed as he realised this must be a replacement horse for CC, a gift from Miranda and Gavin. Otherwise, how would he explain CC's disappearance to his family? He made sure the mare was comfortable before heading back to the house.

As he entered the back door, he whispered thank-you up at the sky.

CHAPTER 31

Learning and Communicating

"OK now it's your turn," Bridget said as she smiled at Cassandra. They were standing outside the Anderson house.

Bridget had just taught Andrew how to transport himself to Centre World, and he had vanished.

Cassandra closed her eyes. Concentrating on a mind image of Centre World, she clasped Bridget's hand and whispered, "Andrew."

When she opened her eyes, they were standing in the lush green grass of Centre World with three moons shining high above them.

Andrew grinned at his girlfriend. "I did it!"

Cassandra gasped.

It was almost midnight. Bridget led the way on foot over to a group of tall, beautiful trees. Bridget said to Cassandra, "As Gods we can communicate with nature by sharing images. Place your hand on one of the trees."

Cassandra glanced at Andrew, who shrugged before laying her right hand on the bark of one of the trees.

After a moment, she said to Bridget, "What now?"

Bridget replied, "Concentrate. Share an image."

Cassandra wondered what she could share with a tree. She closed her eyes and pictured a lone tree she had once seen on a city street when visiting relatives. Suddenly the word *loneliness* formed in her mind. But her mind hadn't put it there.

Cassandra opened her eyes in surprise. The tree stood solid before her. Slowly she closed her eyes again. The words *Do not be afraid, God of Rainbows* filled her mind, followed by an image of many trees waving their leaves cheerily. Cassandra relaxed and smiled. She shared images of times she had spent reading books in summer in the shade of trees.

Bridget asked Andrew to do the same as Cassandra. He closed his eyes and connected easily with the tree.

Suddenly he opened his eyes to stare at Cassandra as her face went white. They could now read each other's minds!

Bridget explained. "This particular tree is ancient with many powers. She has woken your minds to each other and to nature. There is no cause for alarm. Remember you're a match made in Heaven and have no secrets from each other."

They communicated for a short while with each other as well the trees, before Bridget led the way through the trees to a large clearing. There stood a unicorn. Its glorious white coat was beautiful. It turned nervous eyes on Bridget. She smiled politely and kept back saying, "Cassandra, you may approach him."

Cassandra stepped forward slowly, holding out her hand. The stallion stretched his neck forward until he could place his muzzle in her hand.

Cassandra had always thought of unicorns as impossible myths, but here she was patting one! She fussed over him. Andrew stepped forward to pat him too. But the unicorn was a shy creature and only too soon was trotting away in the dark.

Bridget sighed. "They are beautiful but difficult to get near. I don't know if you'll ever pat one again."

Bridget placed a hand over her belly. For a moment, she looked quite faint. Cassandra held one of Bridget's hands and said, "Bridget, I haven't had a chance to say this yet. I'm happy for you and my brother. I just know you will have a beautiful baby."

Bridget's face lit up. She had been wondering what Cassandra thought about her having a baby but hadn't known how to bring the subject up. She gave Cassandra a hug.

"Thank you," Bridget smiled.

CHAPTER 32

Puzzle

Time passed. The replacement CC acted just like the original CC in front of Andrew's relatives and friends. Bridget's pregnancy blossomed. James was fearful of what his parents would think of their fourteen-year-old son becoming a father and didn't tell them of the pregnancy. Cassandra and Andrew became used to reading each other's minds and were doing well in school. They visited Heaven regularly to speak with Miranda and Gavin.

Winter warmed into spring, melting the snow off the mountains. One day Cassandra was sitting with Andrew in Heaven. Miranda said to them, "Have you discussed marriage?"

Andrew's ears turned red.

"We don't like to *r-rush* things," Cassandra stammered.

Miranda laughed, and Gavin rolled his eyes.

"What would our parents think?" Cassandra responded hotly.

"My mother would love it," Andrew muttered.

Miranda smiled warmly at the young couple.

"All we ask is that you think about it," she said.

Andrew took hold of Cassandra's hands. They were about to kiss when a little, white dog suddenly ran up to them. They both jumped in surprise. The dog wagged its tail and looked up at them with deep eyes. Cassandra looked into those eyes and had to look away. Andrew gazed into the dog's eyes, and an image of his family's dogs filled his mind. The dog seemed to make time stand still. Finally, the dog barked twice then ran away.

Andrew turned to ask Miranda and Gavin about the dog. They had vanished.

CHAPTER 33

Less Time

James sat at the piano. He was practising major scales with both hands over two octaves, and he didn't like it. But he wanted to learn piano and his sister insisted he play scales. He looked at Cassandra in annoyance.

She smiled. "You play well," she encouraged.

"Well then, let me play some music! I'm sick of scales." James knew Cassandra loved playing scales, and that made his annoyance worse!

Cassandra laughed. "You need to practise them!"

James finished off a major scale of A, topped it off by slamming the keys down in an A major chord, and then turned to Cassandra. "Can I go outside and play now, boss?" he asked sarcastically, standing up.

Cassandra stuck her nose up in the air. "Well, have you cleaned your room?" she asked jokingly.

James grinned. "Not on your life!"

Cassandra tried to keep up the act but laughed instead. "I give up," she said as she smiled.

Just then, Valery walked up to them with her eyes shining.

"Guess what!"

James shrugged.

Cassandra asked, "What?"

"Your aunty Michelle is getting married! Matt proposed to her last night. He organised a candlelit dinner with champagne and roses. He's so romantic."

"When is the big day?" Cassandra asked happily.

"They're still deciding on that, but they want to be married within two years." Valery looked Cassandra up and down.

"Don't worry, Mum. I won't wear jodhpurs to the wedding." Cassandra sighed.

"Certainly not! Maybe you can wear your hair up too. And some makeup? How about—"

James walked quickly up the hall and out the front door. That was one argument he didn't want to witness. His sister always dressed well, and her grooming was impeccable, but she wasn't as fussy or feminine as their mother wished. He walked out the front door in time to see Ray and Andrew ride up to him on Sun Seeker and CC.

"Is Cassandra here?" Andrew asked. The mid-morning sunshine shone like fire on CC's coat.

"Yeah," James replied. "She's in the house, but I wouldn't go in there."

The brothers looked at James with some concern. James took note of this and laughed.

"It's nothing to worry about! She's just talking to our mother about *girl stuff.*"

Andrew looked away, but Ray laughed.

"How's it going at uni?" James asked Ray.

"Good, although all I ever do is study. It's nice to be horse riding today. Do you want to join us?"

James patted Sun Seeker's neck. "No, I'm meeting up with Bridget. We—"

He was cut off by the sound of the front door slamming. Cassandra stormed up to them. Andrew jumped off CC with delight. Ignoring Cassandra's temper, he swept her into his arms. She was about to say something, but he kissed her passionately and she couldn't help but respond in the same manner. As their lips parted, she was blushing furiously, but her temper melted. She took a deep breath.

"My mother," said she, flicking her long hair over her shoulder, "thinks I've got a lot of growing up to do. She wants me to work part-time in her beauty salon!"

Ray, James, and Andrew grinned at her.

"This means I'll have to wear makeup and—" She glanced around at their faces and saw their amusement. She glared at them.

"And actually work?" James finished her sentence.

Ray and Andrew laughed.

"I think it's a good idea," Andrew assured her.

"Think of the money," Ray put in.

Cassandra started to smile, but her brother couldn't help saying, "Say goodbye to your weekends!" with a grin.

There was a silence. James realised the Anderson brothers didn't like his last comment. It meant there would be less time to spend with Cassandra. He felt sheepish and apologised before slipping away. He made his way to the back of the house.

And there stood Bridget, Dave, and Brendan. They looked uncomfortable about something. James focused on Dave, a good mate in school, but they hardly ever saw each other outside of school. James had been too wrapped up in Bridget's pregnancy. Brendan was always visiting Earth to be with his girlfriend, Kayla.

James felt some guilt.

Dave looked James right in the eye. "Let's do something today, all of us as friends. I'm sick of being left out!"

James shifted his weight. He felt awful. But then he smiled at his unpredictable fun-loving friend.

"Sure. Have you got plans?"

A slow grin spread across Dave's face.

CHAPTER 34

Friends, Fun, and Mandy

"All right!" Dave yelled out of a four-wheel drive window as Bridget drove the vehicle through bushland.

Dave believed the car belonged to Bridget. She had created it with her magic just for him. It was a bumpy dangerous ride, but they were having a great time. A song called "Fun, Fun, Fun" blasted from the stereo. Bridget brought the car to a stop near Cliff Edge, almost giving the guys whiplash.

They were too high-spirited to mind. They all got out of the car to stretch their legs.

Dave thanked Bridget, who shrugged and smiled. "You don't make much of a tour guide," Dave joked.

"I'm surprised you didn't have the baby during that bumpy ride!" Brendan laughed.

Bridget went red. She looked at James, who looked at Dave.

"Um, Bridget and I are having a baby," James said. He had been meaning to tell Dave.

James waited for an outburst, but Dave simply dropped his mouth open. Stepping forward, he took hold of Bridget's hands.

"Should you be driving?" he asked with concern.

Bridget stared at him. "Why not? Of course, I should drive. Now come on. Let's go into town. I'm starving."

"Congratulations! You're not even showing," Dave said as he hugged Bridget. Then he slapped James on the back. *"Daddy,"* he taunted.

James pulled a face.

They got back into the car. Dave got in the back and then reached forward to turn up the stereo as a song came on that suited him: "I Can't Get No Satisfaction." He started singing. They rolled their eyes and told him not to give up his day job. His singing was terrible! He pointed out that he didn't have a day job before sitting back to annoy them with silly jokes. James laughed. Life was never boring with Dave around.

When they arrived in town, the car was scratched and muddy, but they didn't concern themselves with that. They gorged themselves on pasta salad and an apple pie in the local cafe instead.

Then Dave spread four movie tickets on the table in front of him. "Let's go see the new horror movie," he said as he grinned, somewhat maliciously. "I bought these this morning for all of you." He handed out the tickets. They accepted cheerfully.

When they walked into the old movie theatre, they headed straight for the Candy Bar.

Bridget held up some money. "My shout," she announced. "What would you all like?"

Dave looked at her in surprise. "You have everything!" he exclaimed. "Car, money, music from bands most people haven't heard of. How do you do it?"

Bridget glanced at Brendan. Both of them visited Earth regularly, and it was there they found great music. The car and money were from Bridget's magic, but of course she couldn't explain all that to Dave. She was wondering how to get out of this predicament when Brendan nudged her and pointed out a girl standing a few feet away from them.

"Look, Dave. There's Mandy from school," Bridget said quickly, pointing her out to Dave.

"Yeah, but—" Dave's voice trailed off as he turned his hazel eyes from Bridget to see Mandy White standing with her friends. Dave was known for chasing girls but had had a crush on Mandy for the last few weeks. He stood in line watching Mandy, forgetting about Bridget, who breathed a sigh of relief.

Bridget bought soft drinks, popcorn, and miniature jumble cakes for all of them. When they took their seats in front of the movie screen, Bridget waved hello to Mandy and her friends, Nicky and Cheri. They responded by moving from the middle row of seats to the back row to sit with her. They chatted, and by the time the movie had started, everyone had swapped seats so that Dave was beside Mandy.

Mandy was a pretty girl with fair skin and shoulder-length blonde hair. She was a little chubby. She loved shopping, parties, horror movies, swimming, and being out with friends. She was a good match for Dave, and he was intent on letting her find this out.

They all enjoyed the movie. The fact it was a horror didn't worry them in the least. Dave whispered funny things to Mandy throughout the movie and shared his drink with her. She realised he liked her and felt happy.

When the movie finished and the lights were coming back on, they were kissing. The new couple walked out of the movie theatre holding hands. Bridget showed off her car to Nicky and Cheri. They asked for a ride in it, so they all piled in and off they went again.

CHAPTER 35

Decision

"Goodbye!" Cassandra called as Ray turned Sun Seeker and headed home for more study. She stood with Andrew on her parents' property while holding Jet's reins. As soon as Ray was out of sight, CC relaxed and pushed her muzzle into Andrew's hand.

"I have nothing for you," Andrew said as he playfully pushed the mare's nose away.

Cassandra stared at CC. "Was that affection?" she asked in disbelief.

"Yes. I told you this is CC's replacement. Finally, she can let you see. This CC has none of the vices the original CC had."

The lovely chestnut mare stepped towards Cassandra with her ears forward. Cassandra patted her absently.

"She has a beautiful temperament," Andrew said happily.

"Whose dog do you suppose that was in Heaven the other day?"

Andrew shrugged. "I wish I knew! He shared an image of my dogs with me. His eyes showed intelligence. He was puzzling."

Andrew looked off into the distance. Clouds moved slowly across Bridget's beautiful blue sky. Rolling green hills met the foot of the Casyarna Mountains that rose majestically to the sun. Amid all this peace and beauty, Andrew felt worried. Over the past few weeks, he had come to realise he really was a God.

Cassandra was not only his girlfriend but his soul mate. Reality was settling in, and he had to make a decision.

Cassandra watched emotions flicker across Andrew's face. She tensed as she read his last thought; he really did want to be a God.

Andrew took her hand, looking directly into her eyes. Before he could say anything, Cassandra said, "We still have next year to decide," and dropped her eyes.

Andrew let go of her hand. He placed a finger under her chin and lifted until his deep-brown eyes met with her rainbow eyes.

"Time quickly passes, Cassandra. I'm not going to wait until the last minute to work out a decision like this! Gods or mortals? We need to discuss—"

Cassandra's eyes filled with tears. Andrew ceased talking. He was tense, feeling worked up and frustrated.

Both were prone to anxiety; their emotions often ran wild. They were both still coming to grips with the idea of being Gods.

Suddenly Cassandra mounted Jet. She urged him into a gallop towards the mountains.

Andrew calmed down. He leaned up against CC as the mare grazed, watching his hot-tempered love run free. But she wasn't free any more than he was. He took his glasses off and wiped a hand across his eyes.

What were they going to do?

CHAPTER 36

Daddy

Bridget faced James. "We have to let your parents know," she said calmly as she watched James flinch.

"I know," he responded, resigned.

It was a Sunday, one week after his fifteenth birthday. James had finished year 9 and Bridget had finished year 12. A new year wasn't far away, and Bridget was large with child due to be born this summer. It was time to let John and Valery know of the baby, but James was dreading the confrontation. James and Bridget walked into James's house.

It was mid-afternoon and Cassandra and Valery had just arrived home from the beauty salon. Cassandra was used to working at the salon. She picked up on the computer and paperwork quickly and wasn't shy when answering the phones. She got along well with the other ladies who worked there. Her bank balance was steadily growing. Both she and her mother were in high spirits.

They had done some grocery shopping on the way home. They chatted as they stocked the fridge and fruit bowls.

John swept into the kitchen, his black coat billowing behind him. He had won a difficult court case that day. He presented Valery with a bunch of beautiful wildflowers and kissed her passionately.

James walked in just in time to witness the kiss. Cassandra smiled at her brother and shrugged.

"Uh, Mum?" James began.

His parents half turned to him.

"I have something to tell—to show you. Please come into the lounge room," he said. "Bridget is here."

This got his parents' attention. They hadn't seen Bridget for weeks. Whenever they tried to talk to James about her, he clammed up. They had been curious for a while.

Everyone walked into the lounge room. Slowly Bridget stood up. She opened the long, dark coat she was wearing and placed one hand on her pretty red blouse that was covering her pregnant belly. James stood beside her and held her other hand.

Valery was surprised to see the pregnancy revealed. Seeing as Cassandra already knew of the baby, she decided to leave her parents alone with the young couple. She went to play classical music on the piano. John and Valery sat down.

"I'm going to be a father," James said quietly.

John stared at him. "I can see that."

Bridget smiled at James's parents.

"I know this is a shock," she said. "How do you both feel?"

"Worried!" Valery said straight up. "James isn't even finished with school yet and he's becoming a father! What were you both thinking?"

James and Bridget glanced at each other. They hadn't really thought much. Act first. Think later!

John sighed. "I hope you know what you're doing, son. Maybe you should get a part-time job on one of the properties around here. You'll need the extra money."

James nodded.

"What about your parents, young lady?" Valery asked Bridget.

"They're fine with this," Bridget said, although she wasn't completely sure.

Valery's face softened. Standing up, she embraced Bridget.

"Congratulations, Bridget. You're going to be a mother! This is a shock, but I want you to know you're welcome in this family. There's no need to hide anything from us."

Bridget smiled happily and thanked Valery. John stood up and clapped a hand on James's shoulder.

"Come with me, James Terence," John said as he steered his son into his study.

John sat in his huge, black, leather chair behind his enormous desk. Law books lined bookshelves from floor to ceiling behind him. James stood facing him from across the desk, realising what an imposing figure his father cut.

John leaned forward with his hands clasped. "Son, I want you to know that I had already guessed Bridget was pregnant."

James hunched his shoulders miserably. His father leaned back.

"Like father, like son. We look alike, we have the same mannerisms, and you want what I did at your age. Your mother and sister might still be getting to know you, but I'm not. You may be determined, strong, and good at hiding things from people, but not from me. I wish you had told us of the baby sooner. We have been loving, supportive parents. Now we are to be grandparents."

John's face softened slightly. After a short silence, he asked, "Do you love Bridget?"

"Yes," James answered without hesitation under his father's serious gaze.

"Are you going to grace the family and ask for her hand in marriage?"

"Yes," James answered again without hesitation. Then his mouth dropped open in surprise.

John smiled in amusement and stood up.

"Your mother and I can see the love you both share and we like Bridget. Get yourself a job and buy her a ring. Hop to it, *Daddy*."

James groaned at the term *Daddy*. His father grinned at him.

CHAPTER 37

The Angel

James got a job mucking out stables on a neighbouring property. He enjoyed the early mornings and the physical work. The property was used for breeding and breaking in Appaloosas. It was the same place John and Valery had bought Jet for Cassandra.

One morning, James was just finishing up work when Brendan suddenly appeared in front of him. James jumped in surprise.

"You have to come with me," Brendan said.

"OK, let me just put away—"

"Now," Brendan grabbed James's shoulder and they vanished.

Bridget was in labour. She lay in Heaven with three Angels to assist the birth. Beads of sweat lined Bridget's brow as she pushed and breathed under the Angels' instructions. She cried out James's name just as he appeared beside her. Brendan watched his sister worriedly as James crouched down beside her to hold her hand. James murmured encouragement to her and told her he loved her. Bridget gripped his hand hard and found new strength. She endured the labour until an Angel with beautiful dark hair placed a tiny baby girl in her arms.

Bridget smiled as she cuddled her daughter. James's face lit up. At last, he had his own family to love and support. The Angel, ever so peaceful and lovely, started to play a harp. Bridget and James glanced at the Angel, down at the baby, then back up at the Angel. The baby also had dark hair.

Bridget looked at James. "Angel," she whispered.

He grinned. Slipping an arm around her, he agreed Angel was the perfect name for a baby born in Heaven.

"Wings for the middle name?" he said half-jokingly.

Angel Wings she was named.

Miranda and Gavin were on Earth when they sensed their granddaughter's birth. They knew this baby would be special because the father was mortal, but even they didn't know what to expect.

Gavin took Miranda's hand. They were standing in Ireland on a windy coastline. They closed their eyes and transported themselves to Heaven.

CHAPTER 38

Mortal or God?

Gavin and Miranda took turns holding Angel. The baby was healthy and whole, and the proud grandparents lit up at the sight of her. Bridget was feeling sleepy and content.

"What have you named her?" Gavin asked.

"Angel Wings," Bridget replied with a smile.

Gavin froze. Miranda paled.

"What is it?" James asked.

Gavin glanced at his wife then spoke. "This child is part mortal and part God. Angel is a beautiful name for her, but *Wings?* The middle name signifies what she represents to the world! What is wings supposed to mean?"

"It doesn't matter," Bridget snapped. "I don't want my daughter to have godly responsibilities! She can grow and be educated in World of Two Moons, the same as Cassandra. She shouldn't ever have to face Earth!"

Silence greeted her words.

Bridget's eyes changed to a stormy grey. After a moment, she went on. "Angel doesn't have to be a God of anything. I want my daughter to have choices like her father. James named her Wings. Wings her name shall be. She is half mortal—"

"No," Gavin cut in. "We don't know how much of this baby is mortal or how much is God. Wings might be a meaningless name chosen by James, or she could be a God of Wings, such as birds or—"

"Or what?" James asked.

Miranda answered. "Something similar has only happened once before in the family, but, well, she could grow wings."

CHAPTER 39

Uncertain Future

Cassandra and Andrew arrived in Heaven just in time to hear Bridget's outburst. They stood watching and listening, captivated.

Bridget's brothers and sisters gathered around their new niece with delight mixed with worry for her uncertain future. Melinda Snowfall, now four years old, knelt and touched Angel's face.

"Angel Wings, I am Aunty Snowfall," the little red-haired girl said, then kissed the baby's forehead. All the aunties and uncles did the same as was the way of their family when welcoming a new family member. Thomas Mineral, age two, spoke clearly as all infant Gods do.

Andrew held the baby. Cassandra watched him light up at the sight of the baby falling asleep in his arms. She smiled, realising he would love to be a father, yet he would probably not admit it. She walked over to Miranda and took hold of one of the older woman's hands to lend comfort.

Gavin shook his head at his eldest daughter. "What will we do with her? What will she get up to next?" he muttered.

"Why is Bridget against Angel visiting Earth?" Cassandra asked as Andrew tore himself away from the baby and joined his girlfriend.

"Well, Earth can appear similar to your world, but there is much more hardship. Both of you will find out what it's like there. You will have to visit Earth for more learning. Bridget has made friends on Earth, and often she has fun there. She just wants to shelter Angel from the horrors and suffering Earth provides for some people." Miranda sighed. "It's really up to Angel what happens in her future. She is part God after all."

Moving away from the Rosewell family fussing over Angel, Gavin started explaining Earth to Cassandra and Andrew.

"Earth has many different races of people, breeds of animals, climates, and religions. The planet is an exceptionally beautiful, sensual place where peace and happiness can be found, but there are also war, disease, terrorism. The list is endless."

They stopped walking. Gavin and Miranda faced the young couple.

Gavin spoke again. "Being a God means people believe in you without seeing you. You will hear their prayers and forgive their sins. Their pain can become yours. Becoming Gods, you will both have to accept Earth as well as World of Two Moons."

Miranda said, "We wish for Brendan to show you Earth now that you're on school holidays with time on your hands. We all like to visit Earth and World of Two Moons to keep an understanding of what people are going through."

"I thought Gods knew everything," Cassandra said without thinking.

Miranda glanced at Gavin, who smiled at Cassandra. "We learn as we go," he said gently.

Cassandra blushed. She was a God, but she knew very little.

"Where do we go on Earth?" Andrew asked.

"Australia, a land built on by convicts."

"Convicts?"

"People guilty of crimes such as stealing. They were shipped from other countries to Australia. Their punishment was to build bridges and buildings. On good behaviour, they could be freed to live on Australian soil."

Cassandra stared at him. "The country is full of crooks?"

Gavin smiled.

"You will meet Kayla Ocean as well Adam Storm and Damen Lifeblood. All three know they are Gods and visit Heaven regularly. Kayla has decided to become a God. Adam and Damen still face the decision. They live west of Sydney in the State of New South Wales," Miranda said.

Andrew grinned in anticipation, his imagination running wild.

Cassandra smiled uncertainly. Nervously she waited for future events to unfold.

PART 3
REALITY

CHAPTER 40

New South Wales

Brendan took Cassandra and Andrew to the beautiful Blue Mountains to see the sun set. They stood on a lookout near three mountains named the Three Sisters. They watched many birds, such as cockatoos, magpies, rosellas, and galahs, flying all around. Cassandra's eyes were drawn everywhere: the jagged tops of the mountains, the vibrant birds, the valley views, and the tourists with their nonstop chatter and flashing cameras.

That evening, they caught a country train heading to Sydney, New South Wales's capital. The train was fast with limited stops. At Parramatta Railway Station, Brendan changed trains to show them a tangara. This train had some graffiti on the walls that shocked Cassandra. By using a black Texta, someone had changed a sticker from "At night travel near the guard's compartment marked with a blue light" to "At night rave near the guard's compartment naked at night with a blue light."

They arrived in Sydney safely. Brendan showed them the splendour of the city lights, the Harbour Bridge, and the Opera House. They then went to Darling Harbour to a dessert café where they had pancakes, syrup, and ice cream. Cassandra and Andrew enjoyed themselves until Brendan took them to Kings Cross. Here they walked the crowded streets trying not to let their faces drop as scantily clad prostitutes strutted their stuff. Cassandra looked into the eyes of one and saw suffering. They walked past men in suits who tried to lure people into noisy strip clubs.

The next day they visited a suburb west of Sydney at the foot of the Blue Mountains. They met up with Kayla, Damen, and Adam as they hung out with teenage friends by the Nepean River. The group smoked, drank, and tried to outwit each other with funny remarks. The boys wore ripped jeans, offensive T-shirts, and flannelette long-sleeved shirts. The girls wore tiny skirts showing off tiny figures. Cassandra thought their skirts should be longer. Some of them complained about being hungry or bored but did nothing other than sit there. They spoke of things such as "grass," wagging, and dropping out of school or relationships. At the mere mention of parents, shocking language escaped their lips.

Damen Lifeblood seemed to be the worst of the lot, loud with a wicked sense of humour. But he was extremely good-looking and confident. The girls fell for him easily. He could handle difficult situations smoothly. He had been physically abused from birth, causing him to be a survivor. He wouldn't willingly hurt a thing; however, it was advised to stay out of his "bad books." A strong leader and fun to be with, people often vied for his attention, except the parents of teenage girls!

Kayla Ocean used to smoke but stopped when she fell head over heels in love with Brendan. Just like Cassandra and Andrew, they were a match made in Heaven. Kayla and Brendan sat close together under the bridge that day beside the river. Kayla was a shy, quiet girl. She excelled at swimming and gymnastics. Babysitting was a favourite pastime of hers; she had always wanted at least five children! She was quite good friends with Adam and his sister, and it was through them she had made friends with this group.

Adam Storm was a very good friend of Damen's. Together they had drunk Jim Beam alcohol for the first time, dropped out of high school, and stolen cars, only to find out they were born Gods! Whereas it was easy for Kayla to agree to be a God because of her love for Brendan, Adam and Damen thought the whole thing was a laugh. They were known as *Westies*. They had sinned time and time again! Gods? No way! They had been to Heaven and had discovered some powers, but sometimes it was all too much. Unbelievable. Just plain amusing.

One of the guys in the group was an eighteen-year-old named Matt. He lived in a caravan with his father, who was nearly always down the pub. Matt invited everyone into the caravan for drinks. They settled down around the lounge room. AC/DC blasted from Matt's stereo.

Damen and one of the girls disappeared into a bedroom. Matt handed out glasses of beer and joked, "What else is dole money good for?"

Two of the girls, Tash and Jen, wrestled one of the boys down on a lounge chair to pierce his ear. He wanted an earring but knew his father would kill him! He escaped the two girls but lost some blood. By this time, Cassandra had had enough, whereas Andrew didn't mind this kind of entertainment, as long as he wasn't involved! Nevertheless, he excused them both. They walked outside and transported themselves back home to World of Two Moons.

CHAPTER 41

Damen

Damen lay in bed at Matt's place beside a teenage girl. They had just had sex, but he didn't feel too good about it. Since visiting Heaven and talking to people about life, Damen had woken up to reality. He was turning eighteen soon and was facing the fact of becoming a responsible adult. He turned to look at the slender form beside him, not knowing this girl. A *redhead?* Who knew? She dyed her hair. But from their last act, she could be pregnant. He knew the Gods were worried about the new baby Angel, but at least they were sure of Bridget's and James's love.

The cheeky teenage girl rolled a cigarette for him, licking the paper in a sensual way. Damen turned on his most charming smile but felt sick inside, tired of teasing games with girls he wasn't in love with. The girl thought she could melt beside this young man, but only for his good looks and muscles. She was the type to use guys either for attention or other selfish purposes. She had told Damen she was eighteen, working, and on the pill to prevent pregnancy, but she was barely sixteen. They shared the cigarette before going into the caravan lounge room for more social fun and alcohol.

But Damen grew quiet, reflecting on his life. All he knew was abuse, mainly from his resentful parents. He was going nowhere, no education, no family, no money, no loving girlfriend. Discovering his powers in Heaven had encouraged him to enjoy life more. He wasn't religious but was starting to face the fact of being a God. Suddenly his decision was made.

Adam looked into Damen's eyes. They had known each other since primary school. Damen was like an open book to him; he didn't need to read his mind. Adam had also decided to be a God because he liked having powers. Together they left the caravan to transport themselves to Heaven, where they told Miranda and Gavin of their decision to be Gods.

CHAPTER 42

Time Flies

In two years, Cassandra and Andrew finished year 12. They decided to be Gods and were married at the age of eighteen. They met with other God families such as the Goldwells and discovered the little, white dog was named Puzzle, an ancient mystery even Miranda and Gavin couldn't explain or solve. The dog could take on many forms and help people where necessary, and could take on human form.

Cassandra's aunty married Matt but unfortunately couldn't have children. She was a willing babysitter though; Cassandra and Andrew had seven daughters! Cassandra was a practical and loving mum. Andrew was a proud, doting dad. They named their daughters Charissa Spring, Cynthia Autumn, Claire Winter, Corrinne Summer, Casey Island, Cathleen Country, and Celia Earth. They were Gods, and all seven were happy in their childhood. They were being raised fully aware of being Gods but keeping this secret from their grandparents, John and Valery.

Cassandra and Andrew had a romantic, beautiful, expensive wedding, but Bridget and James eloped! This didn't surprise Bridget's parents in the least. James's mother was disappointed because she missed out on a wedding but was happy for them to be together. Bridget had a baby boy and named him Zachary Jonathan. They liked to call him Zac. Bridget and James remained a passionate, fun-loving pair. Their two children were bright, active, and confident. They both had their father's dark hair and eyes.

Angel discovered a few powers, such as making dropped crumbs lying on the lounge room floor vanish before being caught by her parents. At the dinner table, she could pass the milk without using her hands. Her parents made it clear she must never use magic when mortals were around. Whenever they reminded her of this, Angel would pout but behave. Sometimes for fun she would use her magic to create soft, white feathered wings for her back and run around playing "Angels" or "Fairies." Bridget's parents would glance at Bridget with disapproval, but Bridget would give one of her predictable shrugs and of course smile.

James was an involved, loving father. He had always hated the term *Daddy* but loved it when Angel called him that. He taught his children many things, such as fishing, playing piano, and how to stand up for themselves. He wanted them to be caring, confident people. They lived in a new house that was built at the back of John and Valery's house next door to Cassandra and Andrew's new house.

Cassandra's daughters were quiet and girly. They had shy smiles, but there was confidence brimming underneath. Angel would try to liven them up, but all they wanted to do was read in the sunshine while wearing sunhats, bake jumble cakes, or play classical music, such as a Mozart symphony or Beethoven's "Fur Elise" on the piano. Angel wanted to learn karate, play softball, or plan parties. Anytime that Angel went horse riding, she just wanted to race others at a flat-out gallop.

Cassandra was happy at home with her daughters while Andrew worked in town with his beloved computers, programming children's fun, educational games. James continued to work on the property that bred Appaloosa horses. His boss taught him to break in the horses to saddle and bridle. James was teaching Zac, which was a dream come true for Zac, who loved horses. In his spare time, Zac loved to practise drawing and painting horses with the Casyarna Mountains in the background.

Life was like a fairy tale ending for everyone in the happiness ever after part. Happy children with content parents while time flew. But of course, this couldn't last. Reality was about to unearth itself.

Angel was curious about Earth. She knew her mother didn't want her to go there. This heightened Angel's interest and longing. Whatever was forbidden, she wanted. She was spoiled and indulged; getting her own way was a typical day for her. So the day she asked Bridget if she could go to Earth caused immediate problems.

CHAPTER 43

Angel

Bridget put her hands on her hips and stared down at her beautiful, dark-haired, blue-eyed, twelve-year-old daughter. "Repeat after me, child," Bridget began. "N-o spells. No."

Angel's face darkened. "Come on, Mum, *please.*"

Bridget pushed stray red curls off her forehead. The hot sun of summer beat down and shone through the large window of their navy blue and white kitchen. She placed a tray of biscuits into the oven to bake and said, "Earth can be a painful place, Angel. You know that. Why would you want to go there? You've heard all the stories from Damen and me about war, disease, tragedies. Well, the list is so long!"

She turned to face her daughter. She had hardly ever said no to Angel, and what came next shocked her. Angel's face was a mask of fury. True anger blazed in her eyes. James and ten-year-old Zac sauntered into the kitchen just in time to hear Angel scream, "I hate you! I want to go to Earth! I have powers, and maybe I want to be a God one day too!"

Bridget had always hoped Angel wouldn't want to be a God and had always avoided the subject. This had always made Angel angry, but she had hidden her anger until now. Bridget, gone shaky, met eyes with her beloved husband. Zac looked on. He had no interest in being a God himself, content to follow in his father's footsteps. He glanced at his sister; she was wearing a dark-blue swimsuit. She loved the water. She was selfish and stubborn. How could she be a God? He grabbed an ice block from the freezer and walked away, more interested in what was on TV.

James wrapped his arms around his wife and eyed his daughter. "You cannot speak to your mother like that, little girl. What's come over you?"

"I am not a little girl," Angel bit out.

James laughed. "You're only twelve!"

"Yes! High school next month! Think about that!"

"What's to think about?" James asked.

"I want to go to school on Earth. It's so perfect here, so boring, I don't feel real! I feel as though I know nothing, living in a sheltered cage because of you!"

Bridget composed herself. Her daughter had always known what she wanted and could be very stubborn at times. She sighed. "Now look, my girl. On Earth you could be killed—"

"I'm immortal!"

"We don't know how much of you is immortal! You could be raped, catch a disease."

"Those things don't happen to everyone, and I have some powers to prevent—"

Bridget cut in with "Do you really want to be a God?"

No. Angel just wanted somewhere different, new faces, a challenge, and simply to go where it was forbidden. But she knew the key to Earth was pretending to want to be a God.

Turning on her most winning smile, she said, "Yes, Mummy. Yes, Daddy."

CHAPTER 44

Angel's Way

All seven of Cassandra's daughters were ten years and younger. They understood about being Gods and were already learning their magic. They sat at the family glass dining table while eating tuna sandwiches. Their proud parents sat with them, on either side of the youngest girl, Celia, who was two years old.

"Tuna fish. Yummy!" Celia chirped. She could speak properly like an adult, as all infant Gods can, but refused to, preferring baby talk.

The eldest girl, Charissa, looked at Celia disapprovingly. "I like my tuna fish sandwich," Charissa corrected.

Celia blew a raspberry, causing Cathleen and Casey to giggle.

Charissa finished eating, excused herself from the table, and drifted over to the piano. She sat to play "Rage over a Lost Penny," the famous Beethoven Opus 129, with talented fingers. She then played "Amazing Grace" and "Greensleeves."

After eating, Andrew took Celia and Cathleen upstairs to their shared bedroom for naps. Claire, Corinne, and Casey went to play dress-ups with their mother's clothes, and eight-year-old Cynthia followed her mother into the kitchen to help clean up. Cynthia loved to help people with things. All the girls were well behaved, thoughtful of others, and displayed good manners, but Cynthia was exceptional. She had a cheerful disposition and didn't mind chores, babysitting, or studying. At least her sisters occasionally complained about things, and Cathleen had been known to try tantrums now and then, but not Cynthia.

Halfway through cleaning up, Bridget walked in the back door and into the kitchen. Cassandra could see that her sister-in-law was upset about something and asked Cynthia to go play dress-ups with her sisters.

"Yes, Mummy," Cynthia replied politely before skipping away merrily.

"Is she still the perfect child?" Bridget asked incredulously.

"Yes, she is," Cassandra replied. "Andrew thinks she will snap out of it one day, maybe get a mohawk and a bad attitude, but I hope not."

Bridget watched Cassandra finish the washing up then decided to help by wiping the tabletop clean.

"Why don't you use your powers to do the cleaning?" Bridget asked.

Cassandra shrugged. "I've been brought up to do housework. I don't mind it." She could have gone on to say she liked to set a good example for the children but didn't want to upset Bridget, who hardly ever did housework.

Both women sat down at the table. Bridget explained about Angel wanting to be a God and going to high school on Earth. Cassandra rolled her eyes. Angel always wanted what Bridget forbade. But as for being a God?

"I know she is part God, Bridget, but?"

"We are fairly certain she wants to be a God. It sounds unbelievable, but you should have seen and heard her! We are thinking of letting her go to Earth. My sister Melinda will be doing year 10 there and could watch out for Angel. It will get this out of her system. You know how she is. If we let her have her own way, she will become interested in something else in no time and probably forget about all about Earth."

Cassandra nodded, knowing her niece would get her own way. She was part God anyway; Angel should visit Earth because one day the thought of being a God would be a serious decision for her. Melinda had grown into a lovely teenage girl who got along well with Angel. She would do a good job of looking out for her.

"Angel will be fine, Bridget. Don't worry. It's like you say. She just needs to get it out of her system, which will be in no time."

The adults talked themselves into believing that everything would be OK.

CHAPTER 45

Year 7

Melinda taught Angel how to transport herself to school for her first day. Usually, Melinda would meet up with Sandra, one of her friends, at Sandra's house and walk with her to school, but Sandra was wagging that day.

"But it's the first day of school. She has to be there!" Angel exclaimed.

"Yep," Melinda said as she smiled.

Angel only knew one person in her classes, a girl she had met on orientation day, Tami. Tami had long, pale, blonde hair framing a pretty face. They stuck together like glitter glue the whole day during the confusion of getting lost in the large school between classes and attempting to read their timetables. At recess and lunch, Melinda sat with them trying not to laugh at their fears.

"I've heard about kids getting their heads flushed down the toilet!" Tami worried out loud.

"You're kidding!" Angel said.

"I've heard that the older kids are always out to get the year 7s!"

"Relax, you two. Nothing will happen," Melinda reassured them.

The day was over quickly, but Angel and Tami felt every minute. Both girls weren't keen on spending time in school, but their teachers seemed nice. For the first few months, they were well behaved, but that didn't hold out. They started to get into trouble for talking too much in class and being smart-mouthed to the teachers. Tami was a flirt with all the good-looking boys. Both girls wanted fun. Their parents were always on their backs, saying, "Study for your test," "Hand in your assignment on time," and "How about actually doing your homework for a change?" Both girls just wanted to talk on the phone or do each other's makeup. They were in trouble one day for talking in detention when the teacher asked them how they could talk so much. Both girls shrugged.

They became popular with the other students but unpopular with the teachers. By the end of year 7, they had a group of friends to sit with for lunch. They were only in average classes, but this suited them fine because they were passing tests. Angel decided to go on to year 8 in the Earth high school near the Blue Mountains. She had a happy home life and was enjoying school.

CHAPTER 46

Angel Chooses Earth (Well, *Robbie*)

Angel's group of year 8 friends were all between the ages of thirteen and fifteen. One of them, Suzanna, had repeated year 7 and was slightly older than the rest. She was very much into sports like Angel and always got her own way. Every year she would ask her parents for a considerable amount of money for new clothes, and she usually got the cash. Her parents were divorced, and she loved the fact her daddy was wrapped around her little finger. Angel had always thought *she* had *her* father wrapped around her little finger, until she met Suzanna!

One of the girls was very quiet; her name was Martina. She was bright in class and pleasant to talk to, but she wouldn't open up to anyone about her feelings or home life. Angel often wondered about her, so quiet all the time while the rest of the group was boisterous. Perhaps Martina couldn't get a word in edgewise. The group always had designer-label shoes, clothes, and schoolbags, but not Martina. Martina was their mystery girl. She usually had her nose in a book, but she was genuinely a nice, sweet girl who always said the right thing to not upset anyone.

Angel and Tami went out with the boys in the group off and on. Tami would sometimes flirt with the boys getting their hopes up. Angel thought this was awful! The boys often got their own back though. The girls would dream about meeting up with famous singers or handsome actors, and the boys would say things such as "As if they would be caught dead with any of you!" This usually got the girls annoyed. The boys loved stirring the girls up.

They all liked to listen to music. The only musician among them was Daniel. He played piano and guitar. He had a much younger brother named Christopher he usually stirred up for fun. He always had stories for the group about Christopher, like the time he put him in a shopping trolley and went running up and down the supermarket aisles, much to the discontent of their mother!

Joanna could sing and was in a band for a short time. She didn't mind singing on stage, but when the group asked her to sing on the school grounds, she would get self-conscious and clam up. They used to laugh and start singing badly; they really didn't know how to sing! They would attempt to sing "Eternal Flame" by the Bangles because Joanna loved that song. She was a sociable girl who knew how to enjoy herself. Her eyes were very pretty, clear, pale green that attracted a lot of attention. She was used to people standing around her saying things like "Wow! Look at Jo's eyes!" This could sometimes get annoying, but she was too nice to say anything negative. Joanna never got on their nerves, although sometimes Suzanna would with her sense of humour that wasn't funny. She was quite rude at times! Once they were talking about a TV show called *Happy Days* and Suzanna said to another girl, Maggie, that she would be suited to date the clownish character in that show, Ralph Malph! Maggie was offended. They all knew that Maggie a little sensitive, plus she would like a man in a suit and tie. Suzanna smugly claimed she was only joking. Maggie got her back by saying Suzanna was suited to no one. Everyone laughed, but Suzanna got angry and gave Maggie a filthy look. Suzanna was the type of girl who had to top everyone else.

Outside of school, movies and music ruled their lives. They listened to many bands and would sometimes argue over who could go out with this gorgeous lead singer or that good-looking drummer, etc. Theirs was a fun group, which made up for the fact they had to be in school.

All the girls were constantly thinking about dating and having a steady boyfriend. Martina was quiet and had a shy streak, but she was interested in dating like the rest of them. Tami liked a boy named Aaron; he joined the group in year 8 much to her delight. She got with him in no time, hurting Joshua a little (she had been flirting with him!), but then Joshua asked Maggie out and she said yes. No problem.

Sometimes another student from a different clique at the school would say something hurtful to one of them, and it was always Angel who would stick up for her friend and shut the bully up. Angel was good at turning the tables. The group would sometimes joke and call Angel the leader of their "gang." But they were all simply good friends sticking together.

During that year, Angel became attracted to a very good-looking boy named Robbie. He sometimes talked to Joshua and Daniel. Angel vied for his attention whenever she could! He would say hi to her, and one day he sat next to her in geography class. Tami was infatuated with Aaron anyway, so this left Angel to get to know Robbie. He was an honest, sporty, all-round nice boy. Angel found herself checking her hair and nails and watching her manners for him. He fell for her beauty then found out she was a lot of fun too. She found out they were suited for each other. One day he kissed her. He asked her to be his girlfriend and Angel didn't hesitate to say yes. He would write her love notes such as "Angel, we're made for each other. Love forever, Robbie x."

This of course meant Bridget had no chance of getting Angel to finish her schooling in World of Two Moons. Angel was determined to stay on Earth, World of One Moon.

CHAPTER 47

Martina

One day Martina didn't show up at the school. No one thought anything of it at first, thinking she was sick and would be back in school the next day. But she didn't show up for two whole weeks. Only Joanna knew where she lived.

Joanna approached Angel one day at recess, obviously upset. Just before biting into a shiny red apple, Angel asked Joanna what was wrong. Joanna led the way to a secluded corner of the schoolyard.

"I'm worried about Martina," Joanna began. "She's been away from school for two weeks! Something could be wrong!"

Angel smiled. "Don't worry. She's probably got the chickenpox or something. It takes a while to get better. Remember last year when Suzanna caught chickenpox? Took a couple of weeks to go away. She scratched the spots. She hated every minute!"

"No, Angel! I'm worried because I've been to Martina's house once before and I know she doesn't have a happy home life. Something could have happened to her!"

So far, Angel had only heard Earth stories but not experienced anything tragic. She suddenly realised she was probably about to have her first lesson.

"I want you to come to Martina's house with me," Joanna said. "But don't tell the others. Not even Tami."

"What? Tami is my best friend! I have to tell her!"

"Can you come with me? I don't want to go alone! You're the only one I can trust to keep your mouth shut. Martina doesn't like anyone seeing where she lives or meeting her stepfather."

Angel could see that Joanna was genuinely upset and that Martina might need help. "Why are you asking me? What about Maggie?"

"Maggie can sometimes blab. Are you going to help me or not?"

"Of course." Angel felt she had no choice but wanted to help. "We can go now."

Angel nearly dropped her apple. "What about school?"

Joanna was too upset to care about school that day.

"We have to go now, Angel!"

They sneaked out a back gate of the school without being caught by any teachers. Joanna led the way to Martina's house, which was out of town on a small property nearly an hour's walk from the school. The property was overgrown with weeds. The house was old and shabby, in dire need of paint. The sky was overcast that day, making the place seem even worse. Joanna crept around the side of the house to Martina's bedroom window. At first Angel thought it was weird they didn't just knock on the front door, but she kept her mouth shut feeling the gravity of the situation.

Joanna slowly stood up from a crouching position to look in the window. Martina was lying on her side on the bed, crying and covered in bruises. Her long, dark hair fanned her thin pillow. There was the sound of the front door slamming. Her stepfather was leaving the house. Joanna heard the car start up and move off down the road. This was her chance.

Joanna knocked on the window. Martina jumped, startled, and looked up fearfully. Seeing her friend Joanna, she painfully got up from the bed and walked over to the window. She had the courage to smash it and climb out, clutching her school bag, and run with her friends away from the property. She didn't like the fact Angel was there and had to see how she lived but was grateful for the familiar face. Everyone knew Angel could keep a secret. It was Suzanna and Maggie she didn't trust.

They stopped at a park to catch their breath. Martina explained that her mother had finally left her stepfather, Don, but didn't take Martina along with her as Martina hoped. Martina was then stuck with the violent stepfather, who would drink, beat her, and then lock her in her bedroom. This way, no one would see her scars. Martina was in tears telling her story. Joanna hugged her.

"At least my mum won't be beaten up anymore," Martina said finally, wiping away tears with a clean handkerchief Angel gave her.

CHAPTER 48

Secrets

Martina stayed at Joanna's house. All Martina could think about was her mother. Her grades began to drop.

Angel started to talk to Martina in school more often. This started to upset Tami. Robbie was a nice boyfriend who didn't mind when Angel sometimes asked him if she could speak with Martina alone. Angel wanted to make sure Martina was OK; she seemed more withdrawn than usual. Martina felt depressed and wondered why her mother didn't come to see her.

"She doesn't know where you live," Angel said.

"She knows where I go to school," Martina replied.

"Maybe she is working on weekdays. She will come back soon."

Martina still didn't like to talk about these things, but she liked Angel, who was easy to talk to. Tami would see them and come over to join in, and then of course Martina would go quiet. Tami wondered what secrets her supposedly *best* friend Angel would keep from her.

One day Tami had to let it out to get it off her chest. She confronted Angel. "Are you through with ignoring me, Angel?" Tami said angrily.

Angel was about to start eating her lunch, but she looked up in surprise at her best friend instead. "What?"

"You heard me."

"I haven't been ignoring you!" Angel protested.

"Is Martina your best friend now?" Tami asked.

"What? No! We just—"

"You have secrets with her though, don't you?"

Angel didn't know what to say. Guilt swamped her. She couldn't betray Martina's fragile trust. Her eyes pleaded forgiveness as Tami's shot anger.

"Well?"

Angel took a deep breath. "You're *my* best friend—" Angel started to say.

"Yeah, *right*!" Tami said sarcastically. "See ya round, *Angel*—not! You're no Angel!" Tami turned her back and walked away.

Angel was speechless and upset. Robbie hugged her sympathetically.

"She doesn't understand," he said. "Maybe Tami isn't a good best friend if she can treat you like that. She didn't even give you a chance to explain! Forget her, Angel."

Angel wanted her best friend back. They kept each other sane when schoolwork got tough and always had such fun together. They had known each other for over a year.

Tami headed straight for a group of girls who often teased Angel's friends, and not in a fun way. Tami mingled easily with them and started hanging out with them to avoid Angel. She even dumped poor Aaron because her new friends didn't really like him. Tami started to smoke and wag school, whereas when she had been Angel's friend, she had studied more to plan a future as a career girl.

Over the next couple of weeks, Angel's friends tried to comfort and cheer Angel up.

"I'll be your best friend!" Suzanna said one day.

"Oh no!" Maggie cried.

"Don't be best friends with Suzanna!" Mike said with a laugh. Mike was the newest member of the group, and he had already sussed out Suzanna's spoiled brat behaviour.

Suzanna shot filthy looks at them before speaking again. "We need a party. That's all. And I certainly won't invite *Tami*. How about it? My birthday is coming up and I have permission from my dad—"

"No surprise there!" Maggie laughed.

"To have a party," Suzanna finished.

"Cool." Joanna smiled.

"I'm inviting some friends of mine that go to another school. They live near me. Should be lots of people there. I'll hand out invitations tomorrow."

Yes, that's what I need, Angel thought. Release the party animal within, enjoy Robbie's company, and try to forget Tami, who seemed to be changing for the worse anyway.

CHAPTER 49

Pressure

Suzanna's father owned an expensive brick house with views of the Blue Mountains. Her party was held on a Saturday night in winter. The house was packed with teenagers drinking, smoking, dancing, and some of them kissing. The party started off with music such as "Funky Town" and "Walk Like an Egyptian" before someone put on a much loved Jimmy Barnes CD. In the backyard was a hired jukebox and flashing lights. Dancers went all out to all sorts of songs, such as "Agadoo" and "Nutbush City Limits," on a paved area in front of the garage, the "dance floor." Robbie and Angel were having a good time mingling and dancing with everyone.

Later that night, Robbie led Angel upstairs to a balcony off a spare bedroom. They stood close together and started kissing. Robbie applied more pressure than normal, pressure with his lips pressed on her, pressure with his body pressed on hers. Angel felt a little nervous but thrilled. Robbie then took her into the bedroom. Angel was shocked; they had only been seeing each other for three months. She didn't feel ready for more intimacy. Robbie could feel her resisting and tried to force her on the bed. She slapped his face. He looked surprised then emotionally hurt. He backed off. Angel sank down onto a corner of the bed. There was an uncomfortable silence. Then Robbie sat beside her and held her hand.

"What's wrong?" he whispered.

"What do you think?" she asked.

"I love you, Angel."

"I love you, but I'm not ready. I—"

"If you're not ready, that's OK. I'm sorry."

Relief flooded Angel, but she knew Robbie would want to sleep with her and he would probably apply more pressure from now on. She loved him and didn't want to break up with him. They were only in year 8. What if she fell pregnant? She had heard of the pill to prevent pregnancy, but it wasn't 100 per cent effective. Nervously she pushed her hair behind her ears and gave him a smile. He squeezed her hand and led her back downstairs to the party. They started to enjoy themselves again.

Around midnight, Suzanna's father arrived and started sending teenagers home. The house was a mess, he didn't like the cigarette smell, and he had to work in the morning. But as long as his little girl was happy, so was he.

Angel, Martina, Joanna, and Maggie were to sleep over that night, along with a couple of friends of Suzanna's who went to another school, Emily and Janice. Angel said a long goodbye to Robbie when he had to leave. The girls then walked into the lounge room to lie in their sleeping bags and watch horror movies while eating popcorn and sweets. They didn't get any sleep.

About 2:30 in the morning, Suzanna made a prank phone call to Tami's house. Disguising her voice with a good attempt at a French accent, she asked to speak to the "bush pig" named Tami before quickly hanging up the phone. She didn't know who had answered the phone at Tami's house. The girls were all laughing except for Angel and Martina. Martina was smiling, trying to join in, but it was such a fake smile. Angel was worried about her, wanting to help but not sure how.

And as for thinking about Robbie and Tami, Angel felt like crawling into a hole to let the Earth swallow her up.

CHAPTER 50

Anger

"Well, little Earthling," Bridget said to Angel one afternoon as her daughter dropped her schoolbag in the middle of the lounge room floor and flung herself into an armchair. "How are things in school?"

Angel didn't want to talk. She was thinking of dumping Robbie, trying to forget Tami, and was upset about poor Martina, whose mother still wasn't in the picture. She was finding it hard to concentrate in school and couldn't stand the thought of all her homework that was piling up. She had an assignment due in two days and hadn't started it. Whenever she was stressed, she tended to bite her fingernails. She hardly had any nails left!

Bridget read her daughter's mind. She glanced at the terrible state of her daughter's fingertips with a shudder. It had always been difficult to make Angel stop biting her nails. Sighing, Bridget gently pushed Angel's legs off the lounge so she could sit beside her.

"Want to talk about it?"

"No."

Typical teenage response, thought Bridget. She watched as Angel reluctantly sat up straight then slumped her shoulders anyway.

"How is Robbie?"

Angel shrugged.

"Have you spoken to Tami lately?"

"How can I? She stopped talking to me! She has new friends."

"I see. How about Martina?"

"Mum, I don't want to talk, and I know how to get you to stop reading my mind," Angel said, a little smugly for Bridget's liking.

Angel stood up, grabbed her schoolbag, and stormed off to her bedroom, slamming the door as hard as she could. Bridget transported herself to where James and Zac were exercising a young brown and white Appaloosa in a round yard. Zac was holding one end of a lunge rein and James was giving instructions. They stopped when Bridget appeared.

"Our daddy's girl needs you," Bridget said dryly to James.

"How *is* my daughter?" James asked, half sarcastically. He hardly ever saw Angel anymore. She had turned thirteen last year, then became moody earlier this year. Bridget kept saying this was normal for teenagers, but he didn't like it. Angel used to always come to him either for fun or advice. Not anymore.

He and Zac finished up then headed home.

James walked into Angel's bedroom after giving only one loud knock. He almost tripped over her schoolbag, which had been dumped on the floor. Angel had "I Love Rock & Roll" playing on top volume and didn't even hear him come in. She liked to keep diaries and was writing in one furiously, sitting on her bed surrounded by a huge pile of stuffed animals she couldn't get enough of.

James sat on the bed beside her, and she jumped. She didn't want to be interrupted while she was writing and made the mistake of telling her father to get out. James switched off the stereo and silence enveloped them for a full minute. She had always vied for his attention before now.

"What did you say?"

"Nothing, Daddy," she said quickly.

"Your mother came to me, little girl; I think we need to talk." James watched his beautiful daughter's face tighten as for once she didn't get her own way. He reached over and took the diary, placing it on the foot of the bed.

Slowly, tense now, Angel put her pen into her pencil case. She stared down at the pencil case, which was covered in scribble. "Angel For Robbie Forever. Maggie For Josh …"

"Tell me what is happening, Angel."

"Not much."

"Your grades this year are worse than last year, and you have lost your best friend. What else? Talk to me."

Angel bit back a temper that had never been any use around her father. She just wanted to be alone for a while! She knew her father wouldn't leave. She started to lean towards her stereo to turn the music back on. James moved the stereo out of her reach. He needed to start communication with her again, not go deaf!

Angel hit the roof. Always one to throw fantastic tantrums, today was no exception. She had a few problems she was finding hard to cope with and finally let it all come out as she cried, punched her pillow, and threw things around the room. She finished by throwing the diary as hard as she could at the wall.

James watched all the carry-on without much surprise but with the guilt of a parent partly blaming himself. He had always thought kids grew out of throwing tantrums, especially by the time they were in high school. He and Bridget had only been teenagers when they became parents and were both too stubborn to really listen to good advice that Miranda and Gavin tried to give. He waited until Angel calmed down. She ended up lying on her bed and crying.

"I'll get you a glass of water," he said. He softly kissed his daughter's cheek before leaving the room.

When he came back with the water, Angel was sitting up and wiping away tears. She felt embarrassed but relieved. She sipped the water.

"I'm sorry, Dad."

"Don't ever do that again, Angel. You're too old! And your poor stuffed animal family. *What did they do to deserve being thrown around?* All we need to do is talk. Life is full of problems and disappointments. Whatever you're going through now will seem like nothing one day. You always used to come to me to talk. Why not now?"

Angel hadn't really thought about it. Her mind was usually consumed with problems from Earth. She wasn't supposed to talk to anyone about Martina, which was how she had lost her best friend! Robbie had been really pushy lately; it made her think he only wanted sex. How could she talk to her parents about that? It was bad enough they were upset about her grades in school dropping. She simply did *not* want to do schoolwork!

"I'm waiting," James said.

Angel looked up at him. "Dad, I—"

"No excuses, Angel. You're getting older remember."

"You want me to talk?" she suddenly asked quite fiercely.

"Yes!"

"Really?"

"Yes!"

"Robbie wants sex!"

There, she had said it. Straight out, pretty much like her mother Bridget would have said it. She watched her father's face go blank for a moment.

"Well, is that what you want?" he asked, not sure what to say.

"No, Dad, geez."

"What then?"

"Should I break up with him?"

"What do you think? What do you want?"

"I love him! But—"

There was a short silence, then James spoke. "Look, I've never known you to do what others tell you to. You always did what you wanted, and so far, your decision-making has been fairly good. Don't let this guy force you into anything. You've known each other—what?—five minutes? Not long enough! Dump him!"

"But Dad!"

"Well, hey, you suggested it first. Come on. Give this guy the flick. Find a boyfriend when you leave school. What other problems do you have?"

Angel couldn't help but smile at her father. She remembered why she had always gone to him. His advice was usually what she was thinking of anyway, and he could cheer her up.

"I miss Tami so much! She and I had so much fun together."

"You can have fun with me. Besides, from the little you've told me, it sounds to me like you have a better time around Suzanna! Still giving her heaps? Stirring her up? How's Maggie? You're still popular in school and you're missing *Tami?* She's the one who cut the friendship. Come on. Give me a real problem!"

By this time, Angel was laughing. Talking really did help. She was lucky to have loving, supportive parents.

"Angel, we want you to go to school here, in World of Two Moons. How about it? We want you to think about it please."

But Martina needed her. How could Angel leave Earth now?

CHAPTER 51

Her Middle Name

Angel broke up with Robbie, and it hurt. He was her first love, first boyfriend. He kept his distance from her. Angel started to sit with Martina and Joanna in classes they shared and still hung out with the group at recess and lunch. One day Suzanna and Maggie got into an argument.

They were discussing middle names. Poor Daniel hated his middle name. It took a bribe of buying him sweets from the canteen before he admitted his middle name was Arnold. Naturally, they all laughed, but in a fun, friendly way not to be bullies. Joanna was really quiet throughout the conversation so Suzanna, who had a nice middle name, pounced on poor Jo.

"Come on. Out with it! What's your middle name?" Suzanna grinned wickedly at Joanna.

"Audrey," Joanna said, giving in with a shrug. She knew Suzanna loved her own middle name, which was Rose. Joanna decided not to ask her about it because Suzanna would brag.

Suzanna laughed in Joanna's face as was her way, upsetting Maggie, which was also normal.

"Can't you be nice to people for a change?" Maggie asked Suzanna.

"*What?* I'm a nice person!" Suzanna defended herself.

"Yeah, right!" Maggie said sarcastically.

"Yes, I am right," Suzanna agreed smugly.

"I was being sarcastic, dummy," Maggie shot out.

"You always bite my head off, Maggie. What's your middle name anyway?"

"May," Maggie said with confidence. She thought her middle name was pretty.

"Oh, like the Rod Stewart song. Daggy!" Suzanna laughed.

"Like I haven't heard that before!" Maggie complained.

Suzanna turned to Angel. "So what's yours?" she asked.

"Wings," Angel replied. She had never given much consideration to her middle name.

Suzanna stared at her. "You mean like the cake mix brand?" she asked thoughtlessly.

"No, that's White Wings, dummy!" Maggie laughed at Suzanna.

Suzanna whipped round to face Maggie; her silly temper always flared over nothing. "Well, Angel wings *are* white!" Suzanna said, trying to top Maggie.

The boys glanced at each other. This was by far the silliest argument yet. They stood there saying, "Eh, *derrrrrr*," to stir up Suzanna. *Derrrrrr* was the word they used to make someone realise how silly he or she sounded.

Suzanna asked Joshua what his middle name was, and when he didn't want to answer, she started saying stupid things to try to make him. This upset Maggie again; she and Joshua were still boyfriend and girlfriend. All the silly things Suzanna said had been upsetting Maggie for too long, building anger within. She stood up, told Suzanna to *shut the hell up,* and then promptly pulled her hair.

Suzanna returned the favour, and before they knew it, they were in a fight. Students from other parts of the vast school grounds came running to watch them. Everyone chanted, "Fight! Fight! Fight!"

The two girls screamed, scratched each other with long fingernails, and tried to slap each other's face. It was a true girl fight, more entertaining than guys punching each other. It was all over quickly because a teacher walked over to force them apart. The other students walked away disappointed. They wanted to see more fighting.

Both girls got detention for two weeks. They had never really gotten along that well and the fight certainly did not improve their friendship. They kept giving each other filthy looks and avoiding each other. Unfortunately for Angel, they both wanted Angel's friendship. Angel felt like a tug-of-war was going on and she was the rope.

Angel was friends with both Suzanna and Maggie, but she didn't want a new best friend. She wanted things the way they used to be, the whole group being friends and having fun with only Tami as her best friend. She wondered if there were problems like these in World of Two Moons. Her parents would like her to believe there wasn't. She thought about the silly argument the two girls had gotten into—middle names, for Pete's sake. Suzanna just didn't think sometimes when she used her sense of humour. But the thought of middle names brought about some curiosity. *Wings?* How did her parents come up with that?

One Saturday morning in spring, Angel was sitting at her parents' outdoor furniture for lunch when she asked about her middle name.

Melinda was eating with them that day. She felt a little guilty and had come over to spend time with Angel's family. She felt guilty because she had finished year 10 last year and not gone on to year 11 and 12. She was supposed to be in year 11 and looking out for Angel in school this year, but the girl at the school who needed to decide if she wanted to be a God or not had already made the decision not to be a God. This was because she had become pregnant to a mortal boy and they wanted the baby. Also, the girl had difficulty using her powers; she felt she didn't have the patience for learning to be a God. Nothing would change her mind. Melinda was no longer needed at the high school, and Bridget had already told Melinda not to worry about Angel. Bridget still believed that Angel would leave the Earth high school behind willingly, sooner rather than later.

Now Melinda watched as Bridget almost choked on the potato salad.

"Your middle name?"

"Yes, you know, you gave it to me," Angel said.

"Well actually, no, your father gave it to you," Bridget responded.

"Oh, thanks, dear." James sighed. He faced his fiery daughter. "Don't you like your name? Angel and Wings go together, you know? Angel *Wings?*"

"Yes, Dad, Angels have wings. I get it. Ha ha. How did you come up with it though?"

"You were born in Heaven. It's a suitable name. That's all. A beautiful Angel with dark hair like yours assisted your birth. Now eat your lunch."

"That's not what I heard!" Zac suddenly piped up. He always overheard everything.

Bridget glared at him, and he went on eating.

"What did you hear?" Angel asked her brother.

"The middle name signifies—" Bridget silenced him with a sharp look. Again, he went on eating.

Suddenly Angel realised her middle name could mean something like Melinda's; hers was Snowfall for God of Snow. Could she already be a God and not know it, like when Cassandra was her age? She had discovered at a young age some powers. Zac's middle name was Jonathan. There was no such thing as a God of Jonathan. But God of Wings could be something.

Bridget and James saw the realisation on Angel's face.

"I have some powers, nowhere near as strong as I would hope. I never believed for a second that I could actually be a God. I mean I've thought about it, but?"

"But now it could be a reality?" Bridget asked softly. "Remember it's your choice, Angel. Your choice. I'd prefer you choose not to, please."

CHAPTER 52

Marie

Suzanna and Maggie made up, much to the relief of Angel. At the end of year 8, Angel turned fourteen. The school holidays flew by quickly with plenty of visits to James's parents as well as to Heaven. The following year, Angel started year 9 in the Earth high school. She was beginning to become close to Martina, who was still living at Joanna's house. Joanna's parents were divorced. She only had one sibling, a brother who was ten years older and had moved out of home. Joanna lived with her mother, who didn't mind having Martina live them.

One day Angel and Martina were sitting together in math class when Martina was called to the administration building. She looked surprised and then for some reason fearful. As soon as Martina left the classroom, Angel asked to be excused and ran out after Martina. Catching up with her, she asked, "What's wrong?"

Martina didn't reply. Every day she thought her mother could turn up at the school looking for her, and she felt that today was the day. She just knew it.

They entered the administration building, and there was her mother, Marie, patiently waiting for her. Martina kept her distance, and Angel stayed nearby watching. Marie tried to hug her daughter. Martina stiffened.

They walked out of the building to get away from the scrutiny of the office ladies working there. Angel followed at a safe distance. Both mother and daughter felt awkward in each other's presence. What were they supposed to say to each other? Marie wanted Martina to come live with her again. She had found another man, a "nice" man this time. Martina wondered what "nice" meant. Her mother had had a few boyfriends before, none of them nice.

After a short time, Martina ran from her mother and left the school grounds. Angel ran after her. They sat together beside a creek near the school. Martina was crying while Angel tried to comfort her.

"Sometimes I hate my mother," Martina admitted truthfully.

CHAPTER 53

A New Best Friend

Over the next few months, Martina met with her mother frequently. She met her mother's boyfriend, Jake, and thought he was OK. He was treating her mother well. In the last half of year 9, when spring started in September with warm weather, Martina moved in with her mother. They were living with Jake in a rented townhouse not far from the school. Martina's grades started to improve again, and her depression went away.

Joanna and Angel were happy for her. Angel started to get back into schoolwork as she moved on from her feelings for Robbie. Martina declared one day that Angel was like a best friend to her. Now that Martina wasn't at Joanna's house all the time, Joanna invited others to stay at her place and become close to Maggie. Angel and Martina became best friends.

Angel thought about her middle name every day. God of Birds perhaps? God of Angels? No. God of Cake Mix? No. Simply God of Wings. What wings? She didn't know. She felt more mortal anyway, which was a feeling she didn't how to put into words, but perhaps she felt this way because her powers were few. Perhaps she wasn't a God at all. Her name was suitable for someone born in Heaven. That was all.

Martina had been living with her mother and Jake for a month when she started to be quieter than usual. She started to withdraw from Angel, much to Angel's dismay. What was happening now? Martina wouldn't open up. One day after school, Angel decided to follow Martina home.

Martina walked into a lovely townhouse through the front doorway. Angel stood behind a tree down the side of the townhouse trying to use magic to make herself invisible, which she had difficulty with. It took all her concentration, whereas her mother could be invisible quickly and without effort. Once invisible, Angel entered the house, which was neat and clean with freshly cut flowers in small vases on every windowsill.

She walked upstairs to where Martina was sitting in her bedroom, pulling homework out of her schoolbag. Martina's bedroom was lovely and spacious. Martina did her homework then went back downstairs to get something to eat. Her mother came home from work and said hello to her. Martina smiled at her before returning to her bedroom to read a book. Jake came home a little later and everything seemed pleasant enough, Angel thought, before she transported herself back home.

CHAPTER 54

Withdrawal

Martina continued to be quiet. Angel didn't know how to help her. She had never been able to invite her friends to her place, seeing how it was in another world. Otherwise, she would bring Martina home with her! Often Angel would try to get Martina to speak about whatever it was that was bothering her, to no avail.

Angel followed Martina home every day after school to see if anything was amiss. For two weeks, everything was fine. Then Angel thought maybe something was happening on the weekend. She got up one Saturday morning thinking about Martina. Slowly Angel sat at the table for breakfast. James smiled at her. He had just been joking around with Zac. Bridget said good morning then immediately asked what was wrong.

Angel shrugged, looking like a dark-haired version of her mother.

"What's on your mind?" James asked.

"I'm thinking about Martina," Angel replied.

"Why? Is she OK?" Bridget asked with concern.

"I don't know. She won't talk." Angel didn't want to eat breakfast. She pushed aside a box of cereal.

Zac grabbed it to have seconds.

"Don't pig out too much, you'll turn into a pig," James joked.

"Oink, oink," Zac snorted.

"Well, now you're exactly like James," Bridget threw in, laughing. "Like father, like son!"

James grabbed Bridget, and she sat on his lap. They laughed and kissed as if they were still teenagers. Angel was used to this behaviour from her parents. She wondered if Martina had ever seen her mother in a happy relationship.

Bridget turned to her daughter. "I have a power that lets us watch people on Earth, see what they are up to."

"Hey yeah, let's spy on people!" Zac said.

Bridget ignored his comment.

"Can we see if Martina is OK?" Angel asked.

"Of course, but eat breakfast first."

"Yes, my little girl, eat up before Zac eats us out of house and home," James said, sliding the box of cereal along the table to Angel.

She picked up the box. She gave Zac a plastic toy dinosaur prize that was in the box then ate some breakfast.

Afterwards, Cassandra joined her mother in the lounge room. Bridget used her magic to find Martina. An image of the townhouse kitchen appeared. Martina was drying dishes whilst her mother had her hands in the sink full of bubbly water. They were talking to each other and seemed happy. The image disappeared.

"She seems fine, Angel," Bridget said.

"But Mum! That was only for a minute!"

"We are not going to spy on them, Angel! We will have another look a bit later on."

They checked in on Martina every two hours that day. But it wasn't until the next day they finally saw what was happening to cause Martina's withdrawal.

CHAPTER 55

Jake

At 2:00 p.m. on Sunday, a terrible image was portrayed. Marie left the townhouse to go shopping, leaving Martina alone with her mother's boyfriend, Jake. Martina was in her bedroom working on an assignment when Jake walked in without knocking. Martina looked up fearfully.

Jake started to speak to her softly, before holding her hand and forcing her on the bed. He stripped off her jeans and underpants. He started feeling her between her legs against her will. Martina cried softly into a pillow. Bridget stopped the image and turned to her daughter. Angel had vanished.

Angel transported herself to Earth. She entered the townhouse, panicky for Martina. She ran upstairs and opened Martina's bedroom door. Jake jumped up in surprise. Bridget transported James to Earth just in time. James, who hadn't seen the image, glanced at the situation, Martina's tears, and saw that Jake was about to make a lunge to grab Angel. Touch his daughter? Think not!

James grabbed Jake round the throat and punched him in the face.

Angel stood as Martina got dressed. James left Jake lying on the floor, bleeding and bruised, before escorting the two girls outside the house.

They went to a nearby park to sit a while. Martina was embarrassed. Angel sat with her arm around her.

"This is my father, James," Angel introduced them.

"What happened?" James asked softly.

"Jake was trying to—um." Angel faltered.

"He doesn't actually sleep with me. He just, you know, feels me." Martina's voice was so soft. She didn't want to admit to anything.

They sat there for an hour before Martina finally opened up. Her mother was so happy with Jake that Martina had kept the abuse a secret, not wanting them to break up.

"I can move out of home one day, and they can stay together. That will be the end of it," she explained.

James was angry to hear this but touched that Martina could put others before herself.

"No way do you have to put up with that!" James said firmly. "Do you think your mother wants a man that goes behind her back? We have to put a stop to this!"

Martina asked Angel how she knew to turn up at the right time.

Angel faltered again. "Um, what are best friends for?"

Martina smiled a thin, wavering smile that disappeared as quickly as it came.

CHAPTER 56

Martina's Note

Martina moved back in with Joanna. Marie was shocked when she arrived home to find Jake beaten up. Angel told Marie straight out that Jake had been sexually abusing Martina. She didn't tell Marie where Martina was living. Marie and Jake began arguing all the time as their trust began to fade.

Angel found it difficult to cheer Martina up. Martina had been abused since she was little and thought she could handle it, but sexual abuse was something new to play on her mind. She sometimes had nightmares in which Jake came to her to speak softly, hold her hand, and then try to force her down on the bed.

Her emotions and thoughts were leading her down a dark path. She didn't know how to stop it. She had heard of teenage suicide and thought she was stronger than that. Now she wasn't so sure. Angel would talk to her and say she was there for her. "Just hold on. Things will get better." But Angel had wonderful parents and a happy home life. Martina had abuse and misery that could last for years. She couldn't hold on.

One school day, Joanna gave Angel a note first thing in the morning on a Monday. Angel's name was written in Martina's handwriting on the folded side of the note. Angel stared at Joanna.

"She left this for you," Joanna shrugged. "I think she is already here at school. She wasn't home when I got up this morning." Joanna went off to her first class without a clue as to what the note was.

Slowly, almost fearfully, Angel unfolded the piece of paper. As she read, tears fell.

Angel,

You are the best friend I ever had, truly an Angel, but I can't keep hanging on. I don't want to be alive with this sadness anymore.

You asked questions that I never answered. How could I answer? I didn't want you dragged into my pain.

My father left us when I was one. I don't remember him. Mum says he didn't want me to be born. I guess that's why he left. After that, Mum had other men. For some reason, they would either beat her up or me.

I hope one day she finds a man who will treat her right.

Please don't blame yourself for my death.

I choose to do this.

Love, Martina

Angel couldn't think straight once she read that note. Martina chose death.

Her best friend committed suicide. It was all over media in no time. At 6:45 a.m. today, a young girl jumped to her death in the Blue Mountains—on a beautiful, sunny, spring morning.

Angel transported herself to where the death took place and cried many tears. She decided not to go to the funeral, unable to face Marie. She didn't know whether to hate Marie or feel sorry for her.

TEENAGE SUICIDE

At 6:45 a.m. today, a young girl jumped to her death in the Blue Mountains. Fourteen-year-old Martina was in year 9. Martina was doing well in school and had a happy home, her mother Marie said tearfully to the press.
"Martina was a lovely girl and always surrounded by friends. We love her, and we will miss her," Jake, Marie's boyfriend, said, his arm around Marie. At the place where Martina chose to die sat a beautiful, young girl crying uncontrollably. Her long, dark hair partially hid her face, and she would not talk to the press.
No one knows why young people choose to take their own lives. Our thoughts and hearts are with Marie, Jake, and all who are touched by Martina's death.

CHAPTER 57

Home Sweet Home

Angel stayed out of school. She couldn't stop crying for days. She had an ache within. Bridget and James did what they could for her. Her fifteenth birthday came and went with a cake and a few presents. Usually, Angel was enthusiastic about her birthday for days before and after, but not this year. Reality was setting in, and with it came some depression. Bridget and James finally talked Angel into staying home, where her family could support her to help her move on with her life.

www.ingramcontent.com/pod-product-compliance
Ingram Content Group UK Ltd.
Pitfield, Milton Keynes, MK11 3LW, UK
UKHW041953230426
12048UKWH00008B/312